"Are you goi[ng
Jessie said wi[th

"Men don't die fro[m] teeth in pain. He felt like he'd been slammed by a wrecking ball—not tackled by a small, curvy woman. "I'm fine, really. Now go!"

As Jessie walked away, Lucas let out a heavy breath, waiting out the throbbing. Jessie was a damn attractive woman. Too bad she had that liberal, bleeding-heart mentality.

She'd only really smiled at him with warmth when he'd been hurt. Probably any man who got Miss Heart-On-Her-Sleeve into bed had to bash himself in the head with a tire iron and lapse into unconsciousness first. Lucas chuckled darkly at his train of thought. What did he *care* what turned that woman on, anyway?

To
Lenore Hunter Roszel
my enemy
my friend
my mother

I love you, Mom

———— ~ ————

RENEE ROSZEL
is also the author
of these novels in
Temptation

ANOTHER HEAVEN
LEGENDARY LOVER
VALENTINE'S KNIGHT
UNWILLING WIFE
DEVIL TO PAY

NO MORE MR. NICE

Renee Roszel

MILLS & BOON LIMITED
ETON HOUSE, 18-24 PARADISE ROAD
RICHMOND, SURREY TW9 1SR

DID YOU PURCHASE THIS BOOK WITHOUT A COVER?
If you did, you should be aware it is **stolen property** as it was
reported *unsold and destroyed* by a retailer. Neither the Author nor
the publisher has received any payment for this book.

*All the characters in this book have no existence outside the imagina-
tion of the Author, and have no relation whatsoever to anyone bearing
the same name or names. They are not even distantly inspired by any
individual known or unknown to the Author, and all the incidents are
pure invention.*

*All rights reserved. The text of this publication or any part thereof
may not be reproduced or transmitted in any form or by any means,
electronic or mechanical, including photocopying, recording, stor-
age in an information retrieval system, or otherwise, without the
written permission of the publisher.*

*This book is sold subject to the condition that it shall not, by way of trade
or otherwise, be lent, resold, hired out or otherwise circulated without
the prior consent of the publisher in any form of binding or cover other
than that in which it is published and without a similar condition
including this condition being imposed on the subsequent purchaser.*

*MILLS & BOON and the Rose Device are trademarks of the
publisher. TEMPTATION is a trademark of Harlequin Enterprises
Limited, used under licence.*

*First published in Great Britain in 1994
by Mills & Boon Limited, Eton House, 18-24 Paradise Road,
Richmond, Surrey TW9 1SR*

© Renee Roszel Wilson 1993

ISBN 0 263 78755 9

21 - 9406

*Printed in Great Britain by
BPC Paperbacks Ltd
A member of
The British Printing Company Ltd*

1

> "It is terrifying to care, of course, and the young man, whom I once heard say to the girl whose hand he was holding, 'Shit. I think I love you,' in the ominous tones of someone declaring that he was coming down with the plague, probably put the fear that accompanies loving as graphically as it can be put."
>
> Merle Shain

"*DAMMIT!* HELL HAD BETTER freeze over soon," growled Lucas Brand, a surge of rage washing through him. "I promise you, baby, before this month is over, Satan's going to have one hell of a head cold."

He'd been warned he was fighting a losing battle, but he'd refused to listen. He'd beat the odds for years and had no intention of losing this time—not with millions of dollars at stake.

But time was running out, and Lucas couldn't remember being this tired in his life. Workdays—that had always been dawn till dusk for him—now stretched into twenty-four-hour shout-a-thons.

He sat at his spaceshiplike work station, testing his latest model of what he'd come to refer to as the Force Feedback Glove from Hell, damning it to a life of mulching gardens—all it was good for—and also damning the fact that the clock was ticking toward the deadline, every second shoving him closer to defeat. He forcefully shut out the thought.

Lucas just had to get this flawed piece of space-age junk to work. No one in the Virtual Reality software business had yet come up with a cordless, force-feedback glove. And he had only fourteen lousy days left to come up with the technology to mimic the feeling of solidity in his brilliantly programmed, streamlined, *good-for-nothing* glove. After all, he had assured Takahashi that his company could create a working prototype by the first of December. If he didn't, he'd forfeit his chance at the contract of a lifetime.

Not one to give up, he reached back into cyberspace and lifted a big orange molecule, squeezing hard. The experimental glove gave him the sensation that the imaginary thing was solid—for a second—then that solidity dissipated, as it had in every test up to now, and he felt nothing—dead, empty air. It was like losing the sense of touch, mid-fondle! Damned frustrating.

"Confound you," he bit out, flexing the gloved hand, or at least trying to. It still didn't work right!

"Takahashi'll love this," he jeered. "His bioengineers are moving a molecule in an unstable compound, the glove goes dead, the molecule drops into the wrong slot, and presto—instant nuclear holocaust." His chuckle was sharp and mirthless. "Yeah, we've got this contract in the bag—if global extinction is the man's goal."

He was hooked up to several hundred thousand dollars' worth of computer equipment via his head-mounted display. Through the HMD he could see his Virtual Reality world, strewn with molecular structures invisible to the human eye. The goal of his VR program was, ultimately, to enable the Takahashi Pharmaceutical Company to move chemical bonds on molecules and "see" how the molecules might react.

Not exactly a walk through the tulips, this was an opportunity to make history. Still, Lucas felt that with his own expertise and that of the two other computer geniuses in his company, he had as good a chance of conquering it as anybody currently in the VR field.

The intercom buzzed. What did it take around here to get obedience—whips and chains? Didn't everybody see he was under the gun? He needed time to think, *blast it*. What could be so all-fired important that his secretary would dare interrupt him?

"Hell, Debbie!" he objected over the intercom. "I told you no calls." Jerking off his head-mounted display, he ordered, "Tell Fletch and Sol to—"

Debbie broke in with a meek clearing of her throat. "Mr. Brand, there's a registered letter here for you. From a Mr. Roxbury. Should I—"

"Roxbury?" Lucas interrupted, his preoccupation with business troubles suddenly short-circuited by a name out of his past.

"Yes, sir. Norman V. Roxbury, Roxbury Enterprises."

Lucas set aside his HMD and stripped off the glove. Sweeping his gaze over his office, covered with printouts and wadded, discarded notes, he muttered, "Hell! After all these years, *not now . . .*"

"Sir?" she replied with confusion.

"Bring me the letter, Debbie. And hold those calls to Fletch and Sol."

Seconds later, Debbie, an attractive brunette, slipped through the double-doored entry to his luxurious, cluttered office. Padding across royal blue carpeting past a massive cherry desk, she halted by his VR work station, quipping, "Beam me up, Scotty."

It was a standing joke, since the VR station looked like a scaled-down version of the *Starship Enterprise.*

Scowling, he groused, "Very funny, as always. Give it to me."

Extending an arm decorated with Native American jewelry, Debbie offered sympathetically, "Hope it's good news, Mr. Brand."

"It's not," he muttered. "It's a long-overdue bill." He got up from the modular seat where he'd been crouched before a monitor displaying raw data. Seizing the letter, he warned, "Even if the place burns down around me, Debbie, no more interruptions this afternoon."

As Debbie hurried out, he tossed the letter onto his desk and grabbed up a printout that was lying across the corner of his work station. Scanning it, he searched for mistakes. After a minute, he realized his mind had drifted away. The letter was bothering him. *Why now?* Roxbury had waited fifteen years, and now, when Lucas had more at stake than he'd ever had before, *now*, Roxbury decided to collect on the debt.

He stalked to the desk and sank into his leather chair, grabbing the letter and ripping it open. Inside was a single sheet of expensive, gilt-edged stationery. On it, in scrawled handwriting, was a message, short and to the point: "Lucas, my boy, I need a favor."

Lucas slammed the paper down. "Blast it to Hades." Even though he'd known, someday, it would come, this was the worst possible timing. Yet no matter how bad the timing, it was a debt that had to be paid. He'd promised to honor The Summons when it came. Apparently, today was that day.

Swiveling around, he jabbed the intercom button. "Debbie, get me Roxbury Enterprises. Norman V. Roxbury—"

"Yes, sir." Debbie sounded surprised. "I know about him. Isn't he that philanthropist they call Mr. Niceguy?"

Lucas inhaled, attempting to regain his calm. "That's the one."

A few minutes later, he'd been informed by his secretary that Mr. Roxbury was at the Oklahoma City General Hospital, in the Roxbury Suite. Disconcerted that Roxbury was ill, but knowing that The Summons meant he had to make an immediate appearance, hospital or no, Lucas left, with Debbie staring after him, her chocolate brown eyes wide with astonishment.

If he hadn't been in such a foul mood, he might have found her reaction amusing. Debbie Windwalker had worked for him for five years. She'd repeatedly expressed concern over his obsessiveness and the fact that mentally he never left work. In all those years, she'd never seen him bolt from the office with a mumbled excuse, leaving no phone number at which he could be reached. It was as out of character for him as it would be for the president of the United States to cheerfully, and for no apparent reason, surrender the Oval Office to the opposing political party.

As Lucas headed toward the hospital in his chauffeur-driven limo, he wrestled long and hard with his conscience. True, he owed Mr. Roxbury a favor, and he planned to repay that favor in full, but Lucas's software company *had to* come up with an economical

Virtual Reality program before his six hungry competitors did.

To make the strain worse, Takahashi was putting the screws to him, having notified him this morning that he was moving up the deadline. Hearing the bad news, Lucas's board of directors was screaming for results.

The pressure was intense, almost physically painful. But Lucas was used to business stress. It was the only kind of pain he allowed himself—pain that would ultimately bring him megaprofits for his efforts. Surely Norman Roxbury would understand his need to delay repaying the favor—whatever it was—for a short time.

Lucas made a tough decision. He'd be gracious, but firm. He would be happy to do Mr. Roxbury any favor he asked. But not now. After the New Year, possibly. That way, he'd have this deal behind him, and he could make a little time to indulge the old man's whims.

Pushing aside nagging guilt, he took the elevator to the hospital's top floor, dubbed The Roxbury Suite— an opulent apartment filled with expensive antiques. Its window-walls offered a panoramic view of the Oklahoma City skyline. The bronzes and russets of the late-autumn countryside beckoned from a distance. *So the leaves are finally turning,* Lucas mused. He hadn't even noticed.

Apparently his foul mood was etched on his features, since the head nurse was staring up at him with wide-eyed alarm.

"I'm Lucas Brand. Here to see Norman Roxbury," he said, feeling bitter irritation over every second he had to spend away from his work.

The woman nodded, her expression easing slightly as she led him through the living area into a huge bedroom. Rich, warm colors and mellow wood furnishings gave the place the opposite of a hospital feel. A big bed, overflowing with pillows and comforters in rusty shades of brown, looked like a gigantic toasted marshmallow, and seemed out of place in a sickroom. In its billowing center, looking small, pale and pitifully insignificant, lay the white-haired man to whom Lucas owed so much—Norman Victor Roxbury.

Lucas winced. Norman had seemed like a jolly, robust Santa Claus when Lucas had been fourteen. Now, he appeared a gray shadow of his former self. Even frail and ill, however, he still smiled his familiar, gentle smile. Lucas felt a rush of memories—how old Roxbury had taken him by the shoulders that day long ago, squeezed and said, "Let's talk, my boy." He gulped hard, recalling the compassion of the man; the way he'd instilled hope in Lucas's broken heart, and the desire to try to make something of himself. Damn. He'd forgotten how much he'd loved— He stopped himself. Sentimentality had no place in his life. Lucas had to take a hardnosed stand, and not allow that elfish grin to sway him. There was too much at stake.

Assuming the deceptive smile he exhibited in business confrontations, he made quick work of the distance to the bed to shake the patient's hand. "They stuck you in a pretty nice room, Norman," he kidded halfheartedly, feeling like a jerk as he looked into those old, twinkling eyes. Why did the man have to be so obviously pleased to see him? It had been years, but he could still feel the bond. If anybody in Lucas's life had been there for him when he'd needed somebody, it had been Norman Roxbury.

Lucas realized, with a sense of depression, that this refusal he was going to have to make would be tougher than anything he'd had to do in a long, tough career.

Roxbury's smile broadened as he replied, "All it takes to get a fancy room like this, my boy, is to donate a wing to the hospital. They'll treat ya pretty good, every time."

Lucas managed a chuckle, reminding himself he was a survivor, not a sentimental fool. He'd make Norman understand his problem. The old man wouldn't die from the disappointment. You didn't die from being disappointed. Lucas, himself, was proof of that.

Troubled by what he had to say, but knowing it had to be said, he plunged ahead, his features reflecting his serious state of mind. "Look, Norman, I don't have much time, so—" He halted, catching movement in a far corner of the bedroom. A slender woman was standing there, partly hidden by a towering ficus. She had straight, sandy blond hair that hung to her shoulders. Wispy bangs skimmed eyes that were focused on him. When Norman noticed Lucas had seen his other guest, he said, "Ah, yes, meet Mrs. Glen. Jessica. Pretty name, but for some reason, she prefers Jess."

Lucas nodded, his half smile reflexive. It interested him to note that she mimicked his nod, but when she returned the friendly expression there was a remoteness about it that seemed to say she was as hesitant about this meeting as he. *Strange*, he thought, as she turned away to pour liquid from a silver pitcher sitting on a marble-topped commode. Before Norman spoke again, she moved silently across the rust carpet with the glass and handed it to Roxbury. Without another glance at Lucas, she seated herself in a nearby Queen Anne chair.

She's shy, Lucas decided. But something nagged. It wasn't only that. There'd been more to her look. She crossed her ankles, and he noticed that the skirt of her slim, brown suit had a slit up the front, revealing very long legs. Good legs. He glanced back at her face and caught her narrowed gaze on him—a gaze that seemed unaccountably provoked. Or was it? He couldn't be sure, for as soon as their glances met, she looked down at Mr. Roxbury, who had cleared his throat.

"Sit down, my boy," Roxbury said, indicating another antique chair that was placed strategically nearby. Lucas was hesitant. He hadn't intended to stay long enough to sit. Reluctantly, he acknowledged he should spare a few minutes. He owed old Roxbury that much. All the while, in the back of his mind, Takahashi and his hundred-million-dollar demand loomed. He took the proffered seat, primed to explain his deadline, and to add his assurance that he would do whatever was asked of him—only later.

Not even attempting to relax in the spindly chair, Lucas asked, "How've you been, Norman?" As soon as he'd uttered the question, he chuckled humorlessly. Obviously fatigue and his preoccupation with work were to blame for such an inane remark. A man in a hospital bed wasn't likely to be in perfect health. "Sorry, I assume you're not here for the haute cuisine."

Norman's laugh was more delicate than Lucas remembered, but the man was in his seventies, after all. Suddenly Lucas had an unruly craving to turn back time, for the old man's sake. He wished Norman were stronger—and maybe a little less happy to see the boy he'd helped so long ago. As he soberly watched, Roxbury took a sip of the water Jess Glen had given him. When he moved to set it on his beside table, his gnarled hand trembled. "Afraid it's practically a cliché, my boy. Fell and broke a hip. Then a pesky stroke complicated matters. I'm doing fine, but the doc says I have to stay laid up here for two or three more weeks to get strong enough for physical therapy."

Lucas experienced a stab of sadness, but squelched it, murmuring the obligatory, "I'm sorry."

Norman chuckled again, apparently unaware of Lucas's unease. "Well, if you've got to be laid up, I suppose this isn't such a rotten hole." He smiled, seeming to take his misfortune in stride. Lucas mused again that Norman Roxbury had the kindest smile. He'd forgotten what gentleness radiated from the old man. He caught himself, and cursed silently. *Blast it*. That smile could make a strong man crumble and children believe in miracles. It could draw a person in to buy whatever wares he was selling. *Let the buyer beware*, Lucas cautioned himself.

Norman was truly kind, wholly good; but right now, Lucas couldn't afford to be affected by his sweetness. He had to keep his wits about him, be single-minded and resolute. Besides, he wouldn't *really* be refusing Norman. He'd only be postponing the favor—whatever it was. He needn't feel defensive or guilty—not even in the face of that grandfatherly grin.

So what, if Lucas had been orphaned and left in foster care, and had been angry at the world, getting into minor skirmishes with the school and the law? So what, if Roxbury had come along with his Mr. Niceguy program, helping kids like him gain the incentive to stay in school and turn their lives around? So what, if he'd paid for Lucas's college education, only requiring the promise of doing him "a favor" one day, in return? He wouldn't be manipulated by that smile. Bottom line, he had people to answer to, a business to run. *That smile be damned.*

"My boy," the old man said, drawing Lucas from his rationalizations. "I have a favor to ask of you."

Lucas went tense, but didn't interrupt. Maybe the favor wouldn't require his immediate attention. Maybe it would be a bequest of money to some charity or other. Maybe he wouldn't have to say no. He waited for Norman to explain.

"You remember the Thanksgiving Dinner and Retreat you attended some twenty-two years ago?"

Lucas nodded, apprehension clenching his gut. Thanksgiving was only a week away. *Not now,* his mind demanded, as though he could manipulate the slant of this conversation by force of will. *Not now, dammit!*

"Well, my boy," Norman was explaining in his raspy voice, "as you can see, I'm not going to be able to handle my Mr. Niceguy project this year. So, I was hoping you could take over for me, with Jess as your assistant."

Lucas's hopes plummeted, but he didn't speak immediately. He had to phrase his refusal as kindly as possible. While he worked it out in his mind, he flicked a glance at the woman and noticed she was again staring at him, biting down on her lower lip. Her expression was taut, and her fingers were beating out a rapid rat-a-tat on the purse in her lap. He couldn't tell if she was worried that he would turn her boss down, or that he wouldn't.

"Lucas?" Norman prompted. "What do you think, my boy? Can you help me out next week?"

The moment had come to gently let the old man down—at least for the time being. Pushing back another sharp twinge of guilt, he gave Norman Roxbury his most persuasive grin, positive the old guy—being a businessman himself—would understand about deadlines that involved millions of dollars in profits. "You know I'd be more than happy to help you, Norman—at any other time. Right now, I'm involved in a deal that'll keep me occupied for the next several weeks. I'm afraid I'll have to pass."

Roxbury's smile never wavered. "I see," he said.

A cough from the other side of the bed drew Lucas's attention. Mrs. Glen's lips were tilted in a vague smile, but there was something unconvincing about her friendly manner. "We appreciate your frankness, Mr. Brand," she commented, her voice throaty but tremulous. "A man like you, who's fought for everything he's ever gotten." She paused, chewing her lip. "Except, of course for your college education. Well, we understand how busy you are. I'm sure Mr. Roxbury can find someone who can free up a little time to . . . repay a favor." She lifted her chin and gave him another small smile that didn't quite gel.

However softly spoken her words, the woman's sarcasm hit home, and that nettled Lucas. He knew he owed Norman a favor, and he was going to pay it back. Only in some other way, at some other time. *Damn, interfering woman.*

"Now, now, Jess, dear," Norman admonished with a wave of his hand, turning to grant Lucas a trusting look. "You'll have to forgive my assistant. She and I have a difference of opinion about your taking on this project for me. Jess preferred to ask Congressman Hillman, but he's served me several times, and, well, he's just had that gallbladder surgery—" Roxbury halted and took another shaky sip of water, then winced.

"Are you in pain?" Jess asked, concern sharpening her words. "I'll call the nurse. It's almost time for your medication."

He put the glass down and waved her concerns aside.

"Look." Lucas directed his comment to the woman. "I don't want to seem rude here, but to be frank, Mrs.— whatever—"

"Glen," she offered without inflection.

"Mrs. Glen," he repeated, dropping his harsh tone. It was uncivil to shout at a woman who was soft-spoken and timid, though it was clear she was trying to be otherwise. Annoyance snaked through him as he realized he had suddenly become the villain here. Deciding to fight reason with reason, he explained, "I'm in a competitive business. I wouldn't expect you to understand the demands of a cutting-edge Virtual Reality software firm like mine, but—"

"Mr. Brand," Jess offered with a self-effacing shrug, "I'm sure I wouldn't understand, so don't waste your time trying to educate me. Mr. Roxbury asked a favor, and you've responded." She looked over at her employer and worry clouded her somber face. "Please don't let us keep you." Facing him again, she added, "Norman should rest. Stress only aggravates his condition."

Lucas eyed her warily, unsure how to react. Clearly she didn't want him involved and was giving him the bum's rush—however demurely. He turned back to Roxbury, who had a sympathetic look on his face.

"My boy," he said, reaching out to pat Lucas on the hand clenched around the arm of his chair. "I'm afraid Jess is rather protective of me these days. She thinks I'll get these old feelings hurt." His chuckle was feeble. "But I told her *never*—not at the hands of Lucas Brand. Not the boy who ran yelling into my pond to save a baby swan from a snapping turtle. Remember? That spring after the Thanksgiving Retreat? You couldn't swim, then. But you never thought about yourself, and you saved the injured gosling—almost drowned doing it. I was as proud of you as if you'd been the son I never had."

Lucas was appalled to see the old man's eyes glisten with tears as he went on, "Never saw anything so noble before or since." He patted again. "Now about that little favor. The Thanksgiving Dinner and Retreat. What do you say?"

Roxbury clearly hadn't taken a word Lucas had said seriously. *Passive-aggressive* was the term that came to mind. Passive-aggressives were the types of people who smiled kindly, listened attentively, and then, by the least offensive means possible, got their way. Norman Roxbury was clearly a master at it.

But Lucas was good at getting his way, too. He hadn't become the president of a multimillion-dollar computer-graphics company by being a dishrag. *Dammit*, he had to say no! He already had too much to do in the next couple of weeks—debt of honor, or no debt of honor.

Uninvited, the memory of that baby swan came to mind. He recalled naming the gosling "Jane," after his grandmother. He'd helped care for her that spring and summer as she'd grown strong again, and then, feeling both sadness and pride, he'd watched her fly away that fall, a beautiful gossamer sight in the clear, Oklahoma sky. From that day, he never saw a swan without thinking of Norman Roxbury—the father he'd never had.

Forcibly shutting out the memory, he responded in a tone that brooked no opposition, "Norman, it's like this—*I'll do it.*"

Lucas frowned. Who the devil had said that? It had sounded a lot like his own voice, but it hadn't sounded much like "no." When he realized he'd just offered to take on the Mr. Niceguy project, he squeezed the arms of the chair so tightly he could hear the wood creak.

What had happened to his famous—no, his *infamous*—control and mastery over situations? *God help me now*, he fumed silently. He must be more exhausted than he'd thought to allow millions of dollars to go right down the toilet. He wouldn't be surprised if his board of directors had him declared incompetent and booted him into the street! Not if he could help it, he vowed. Even though he'd stuck his foot into his mouth and made this idiotic promise, he damn well wouldn't lose this deal!

His gaze roamed to the woman on the other side of the bed. She looked stunned. No doubt their expressions were mirror images of each other. Her fidgety, tapping sounds had stopped. The thump of her purse dropping from her lap and hitting her briefcase was all that broke the stillness.

Lucas cast his glance back at Norman Roxbury, the only person in the room who seemed completely serene. The old man simply continued to smile that gentle, benign smile.

2

JESS STOOD IN THE entrance hall of Lucas Brand's home, shivering. Her parents would have loved this opulent place, but if she had her way, she'd run screaming in the opposite direction. Of course, she wouldn't really. That would be childish, and she was a divorced woman of thirty. Her parents' yearnings and pressures didn't affect her now. Shouldn't, anyway. They'd dragged her behind them in their single-minded lust for exactly this sort of pretension, showing *her* off along with their paintings and trendy furniture. Her parents' pursuit of money had colored so much of her childhood.

As a result, she felt a grudging distaste for any exorbitant show of wealth.

Admittedly Lucas Brand's house was beautiful, yet it exuded a frigid, intimidating elegance. There were no warm, fuzzy vibrations here.

Ahead was a wall of multipaned doors that opened onto a hallway. Beyond that was another set of glass doors that led outside. She was almost blinded by the glittering reflection of the setting sun on a lake just beyond the doors. The fiery glow of sun and water was the entryway's saving grace, giving the house's interior warmth and life. She decided not to credit that phenomenon to either the architect's foresight or to Lucas Brand's direction. She was sure it was merely a happy freak of nature, which she'd arrived in time to witness. The sight calmed her slightly, but not enough.

The butler who had answered her knock had disappeared through the first set of doors and rounded the corner a moment ago. Jess waited, trying not to lose her nerve. Being in Lucas Brand's lake residence—a kind of streamlined plantation house—both awed and upset her, reminding her of old hurts and slights that set her teeth on edge. Her father would have killed to have had an estate like this. Ironically, he'd finally made some big money—though not quite to this degree. But the measure of wealth he now enjoyed was due to Lucas Brand.

Suppressing a surge of bitterness, she reminded herself that she was here as Mr. Roxbury's employee, on Mr. Roxbury's business. She needed to stay focused on that. Lucas didn't know she was related to Clancy Ritter, the man from whom he'd bought a small software firm five years ago to absorb into his own. There was no need for him to know this, and she planned to keep her feelings to herself, for Mr. Roxbury's sake, now that she was *working with* Lucas Brand. A despondent sigh escaped her at that miserable thought.

Nibbling her lower lip, she tried to regain her calm. She'd reread the chapter on "Keeping a Cool Head" in the self-help book she'd bought yesterday, in preparation for this meeting. The title—*Managing Unmanageable People*—had caught her eye. And she'd known Lucas Brand was the pigheaded breed the book dealt with—utterly aloof, utterly confident, with a will of granite and a heart to match.

Though she'd grown up with aggressive parents, she'd never been all that driven, herself; it was a trait her mother and father had tried vainly to encourage in her. At twenty, she married a man who had turned out to be as self-centered and aggressive as her parents. She'd never successfully stood up to any of them—had a horror of dealing with that type—and had become a social-services worker expressly to avoid their sort.

Several years ago, after meeting Norman Roxbury, she'd become fascinated with his Mr. Niceguy program and had asked to be a part of it. When he'd made her his assistant, she'd never realized that one day she'd have to work with the very man who . . .

She gritted her teeth. Enough negative thinking. She had a job to do, and she would have to "manage" the unmanageable Mr. Brand, if Mr. Roxbury's wishes were to be carried out. Though their personal contact had been minimal so far, she'd found Lucas to be the most perverse man she'd ever had the misfortune to come in contact with. He could never be reached by phone, and never returned messages. Finally, in desperation, she'd had to resort to dropping in on him, unannounced. She looked forward to it the way she would look forward to life-threatening surgery—necessary but terrifying.

"Mr. Brand is on the terrace, Mrs. Glen," said the butler, startling her.

"The . . . terrace," she repeated, hoping she wasn't expected to guess where that might be.

The butler, intimidating in a tuxedo, nodded rigidly, and with a small wave indicated the way. "Please follow me."

She trailed along, feeling as though she were being led to the principal's office for some infraction. *No, no, Jess,* she chided herself. *You're a capable, competent*

*adult. You can handle this. Remember, the book says
to "be reasonable, but be assertive." After all, you're in
the right, here. He made a promise.*

They entered a huge living area with a two-story
window-wall that overlooked the lake. That whole side
of the room glowed red-golden with the sunset, making Jess take in a sharp, appreciative breath. The decor
appeared muted in color—charcoal gray leather,
smoked glass—with accents providing splashes of gold
and bloodred.

The ceiling was high, the walls were stark white.
Bold, abstract paintings were strategically hung about
the space, complementing the decor in a way that
seemed handsome and masculine, yet devoid of human warmth—very like her impression of the man who
owned them.

Jess wondered if her father's condo in Florida looked
like this. Probably. Before he'd retired, Clancy had been
very much like Lucas Brand—a cold-blooded businessman. With the five million dollars he'd received
when Lucas purchased his company, her dear old dad
had probably gone all-out with the decorating. After
all, he had a new young wife to please.

Her stomach twisted at the reminder, but she had to
concentrate on the business at hand as the butler
opened a glass-paned door. "Mr. Brand is on the terrace," he repeated, as though he assumed she was too
dim-witted to remember he'd already told her.

She nodded, trying to smile. "Thank you," she
mumbled, as she picked her way down the broad fan-
shaped steps.

Lucas Brand wasn't hard to spot. He stood by the
wall at the end of the brick patio, holding a small por-

table phone to his ear—a tall, black silhouette, solid and substantial against the shimmering splendor of the lake.

Her glance darted skittishly around. A high roof protected comfortable-looking wicker furniture that was scattered about the terrace in conversation areas. Despite the abundance of seating, Mr. Brand remained standing. Jess had the feeling he wasn't a man to sit when he could stand, stand when he could pace, or rest when he could be active—namely, making money.

Now that she was about to confront him, she was so nervous her legs could barely support her. She had no idea what to do, but she decided he'd keep her waiting as long as she let him, so she trudged out to the edge of the patio where he would have to notice her. Her heart thudded against her ribs as she reminded herself she was right to be assertive. Cowering in a corner would never do. Especially with a man like Lucas Brand. If he sensed her fear, he'd attack, chew her up and spit her out.

"You're not serious, Fletch," Lucas demanded. "It's still locking up? Can you get the diagnostics— You already tried? *Hell.*" He seemed to notice movement, and turned, his features in a severe scowl. "Takahashi's going to call for an update in—" he jerked his wrist up to scan his watch "—about an hour. I'll stall him with some techno-bull, but we'd better find the problem pronto. Get Sol back in. I'll be down as soon as I can."

He clicked off, turning to face her with hooded, black eyes. "What is it, Mrs. Glen?"

No, *Good evening, Jess, how's it going?* No *Nice to see you, Mrs. Glen.* What had she expected? Politeness? She hiked her purse strap up on her shoulder more from unease than necessity. It struck her that he looked tired and needed a shave. He was also taller than she'd realized the other day. At least six-four, he was muscular, built more like a football player than a computer nerd.

Computer nerd, indeed! From the first moment she'd met him in Mr. Roxbury's hospital suite, Jess had sensed tremendous energy in him. Lucas Brand wasn't a man who would accept second best at anything. Not from himself or from his associates. From the harassed look on his face, and what she'd just heard on the phone, it appeared he was riding both himself and his employees very hard these days.

"Mrs. Glen," he prodded, his tone weary, "if you have something to say, spit it out. If you're just here for a staring contest, let's make it another time. I'm in the middle of something."

Lucas's uncaring attitude, coupled with her insecurities, filled her with anger. It took all her restraint to keep from suggesting at the top of her lungs where she'd like to see him go. This man didn't care about her problems or about the needy kids in the Mr. Niceguy program—and worse, he didn't care about his debt of honor to Norman Roxbury.

With effort, she collected herself and regrouped, recalling the lesson in chapter two. *Be reasonable, but be assertive*, she chided herself. *Don't blow this, Jess*. Too bad the book hadn't offered step-by-step instructions—catchy phrases, never-fail dialogue. Oh, well, what had she expected for four ninety-five?

She presented him with the toothpaste smile she'd been long trained to exhibit. Every time her parents had paraded her out like some prize poodle, she'd pasted on her "I'm-so-delighted" face and endured the ordeal. It surprised her that she hadn't lost the ability, though she wished she'd lost the necessity. "Good evening, Mr. Brand," she said, extending a hand. "I appreciate your seeing me on such short notice. You have a lovely—"

"If you'll forgive me," he interrupted, "I'm too tired to tap dance. Say what you have to say."

She held fast to her smile, hoping her flinch didn't show, and counted to ten. "Of course. I understand you're a busy man." Belatedly, she realized her rejected hand was still poised before him as though she had designs on his tie. Abruptly she dropped it to her side. "It's just that I've been trying to reach you through proper channels about the Thanksgiving dinner, and, for some reason, we've never connected."

"My secretary's handling that. I assumed she'd get back to you."

"She did," Jess admitted.

"Well, then?"

Be reasonable, be reasonable, be reasonable! Though she was trying to remain civil, she felt her jaw getting tight. "Mr. Brand," she began, "I heard from your secretary today, about the caterer she'd hired for the dinner."

Lucas nodded. "My secretary is very capable. Is that all?"

"Almost." She swallowed to ease a tremor in her voice. "Just one thing. I had to let the caterer go."

His dark eyes widened slightly in surprise. "You what?"

"I—I said—"

"I heard what you said." Lucas thumped his phone down on the wide brick railing. "What the devil did you do that for?"

She lifted her chin, praying her voice wouldn't falter. "Do you recall the Thanksgiving dinner you attended?"

His gaze drifted out over the lake, and his expression softened at some memory. Watching him, waiting for his reply, she had to acknowledge that, even as testy and exhausted as he was, he was handsome, in an unnerving, insolent way. His dark navy suit, white shirt and silver-patterned tie were the epitome of well-heeled elegance. With his tie loosened, and his black hair mussed by the evening breeze, he almost seemed touchable. No, she mused, that had to be an illusion, for there was hard-edged willfulness in the set of his jaw.

"Of course, I remember the damned dinner," he said gruffly.

"Do you remember what caterer Mr. Roxbury hired?"

"No," he ground out too quickly.

"Are you sure?"

He faced her again, obviously annoyed. "What are you trying to say? I have to let those kids make the dinner?"

Though she felt a strong urge to look away from his indignant glare, she eyed him squarely. "You helped make the dinner, didn't you?"

"I scraped pumpkin for pies. What's so earthshakingly important about that? I would think you'd thank me for hiring a caterer. This way, the kids will have more time to play."

"Mr. Roxbury could have afforded a caterer. What did he do?" she coaxed, hoping she was still being reasonable, not playing Twenty Questions. Darned half-baked book.

Lucas said nothing for a moment, but Jess thought she saw a change in his demeanor. Was it a wince? "Are you telling me the old man expects *me* to scrape pumpkins?"

She took a deep breath. "Remember, you're taking his place as Mr. Niceguy."

"It's a waste of time. Forget it. I said I'd be responsible for the dinner, but I'm not going to get involved—personally. I have a meeting that day."

She couldn't believe her ears. "On *Thanksgiving?*"

"I told you we have an important deal, and some problems we have to iron out."

Counting to ten was becoming difficult. Jess dragged a hand through hair that had been tossed forward in a slight breeze, and smoothed it back from her face. The nip of winter in the air helped cool her scorched cheeks.

Before she could form a rational answer, he echoed her own frustrated thought. "Mrs. Glen, let's be reasonable about this—"

"I'm *trying*," she retorted, then stopped herself and closed her eyes, struggling for patience. "Mr. Brand," she began again, "when you offered to take over the Mr. Niceguy Thanksgiving Dinner and Retreat, you made a commitment. I don't doubt that you have a big business deal in the works. I don't doubt that you *always* have a big business deal in the works, but right now, you have a Thanksgiving dinner to plan. It's supposed to be a 'family atmosphere' type dinner, with everybody pitching in. A happy, full day of activity and good memories," she reminded. "Most of these kids have never known family togetherness. We're trying to show these kids a better way, a way they can live, if they want

it badly enough. Can't you see the importance of doing it according to Mr. Roxbury's wishes?"

His eyes burned through her, but he didn't speak. She
knew he was trying to intimidate her with that stare,
and she wondered if he could tell he was succeeding.
But she couldn't let him. This was too important. For
once, she had to be strong, be assertive and stand up to
a bullying egotist. He'd made a promise to Mr. Roxbury and for some unfathomable reason, Norman
thought the sun rose and set for this man. So for her
sweet boss's sake, she was going to be reasonable and
assertive. She was going to show Lucas Brand in a cool-
headed manner, why he needed to do this right. She
would do it if it killed her! Or *he* killed her, a nagging
voice in her brain hastened to add.

With a thin-lipped grimace, the closest she could
come to a smile, Jess motioned toward a seating area.
"Why don't we get more comfortable? I'm sure we can
come to an agreement." Turning away without waiting for a reply, she took a seat in a high-back wicker
chair. She crossed her legs in what she hoped was a
nonchalant manner before she dared face him. He
hadn't moved. She felt a rush of depression about that,
but knew that if he had, she'd have lapsed into a coma
from the shock.

She was at a total loss about how she was going to
wheedle the man into a nearby seat. Besides, she wasn't
any good at manipulation, and Lucas Brand was a
master of it. Who was kidding whom, here? She
couldn't beat him in a psychological battle of wits if she
tried for a billion years. With a sigh, she gave him a direct, honest look. "What, exactly, is *techno-bull?*" she
asked, not quite sure why she was bringing it up. But

the word had bothered her ever since he'd used it earlier on the phone.

He exhibited no reaction to her question at all. She continued to watch him cautiously, wondering what was going on behind that guarded look he was leveling at her.

"What the hell sort of question is that?" he finally asked.

She feared she was getting off the "reasonable-and-assertive" track, but somehow she had a feeling she'd sparked his interest for the very first time. He was really looking at her now, and she sensed he wasn't quite sure what to think. Flying blind, she went with her instincts. "You used that odd term on the phone. *Technobull.* Is that anything like, 'That's a load of bull,' or 'You're full of bull'? Is techno-bull *that* kind of bull, Mr. Brand? If so, I gather you're going to lie to someone tonight?"

She shrugged, suddenly feeling beaten down. "Forgive me if I'm naive. I'm sure you have good reasons for lying. But I need to know if your promise to Mr. Roxbury was . . . techno-bull, too. If it was, I don't have much time to find a replacement for you."

He remained impassive, allowing no hint of emotion to cross his features. Still, Jess had the feeling she'd shifted him off-center.

"What is this tactic?" he asked. "You point out my sins and I'm supposed to atone by being an obedient little Mr. Niceguy?"

She didn't know what to say. Didn't know where she was going with this, so she kept quiet. There was a chapter about keeping quiet in the book. She hadn't read it, yet. She wished she had, because if there was a whole chapter devoted to its benefits, there must be something to it. Girding herself with resolve, she looked squarely into his face and kept her mouth shut.

The hush grew long and strained. Jess was beginning to wonder what, exactly, keeping quiet was supposed to accomplish besides giving a person a neck cramp from holding still too long. She fought the need to tap her fingers on her purse. Chapter one had said that a show of nervousness was a sure way to lose ground, so she continued to act like a statue, no matter how agonizing the act was.

Just as the craving to tap her fingers had grown overwhelming, he startled her by breaking the silence. "Look, Mrs. Glen . . ." His tone was as cold as his stare. "No one in his right mind would tell a potential million-dollar-plus client his program is locked up. For one thing, the problem's temporary. For another, it's bad business to mention every setback. As for my integrity, it's never been questioned."

She felt a shiver along her spine. Why, he was *insulted!* Jess was shocked to discover it was possible to hurt his feelings. Mr. Icy Insolence—who would have thought? She didn't think insulting a man, even such an overbearing one, was anything to be proud of, but since she was this close to actual emotional contact with him, she might as well forge on. "I'm relieved to hear you're a man who keeps his promises," she said without inflection.

He gave her a hard glance, apparently detecting her subtle sarcasm for what it was. "Look. I told Roxbury I'd do the Mr. Niceguy thing. I just won't be as hands-on as he was."

"I see." Jess could no longer keep the animosity from her voice. "In other words, your pledge involved the use of your secretary, your caterer, and probably your servants, but not yourself."

"If you want to put it that way," he stated flatly. "It's the best I can do right now."

His frankness sent her anger seething very near the surface, and her attempt to remain reasonable was quickly going up in smoke. She'd had it up to her eyebrows with self-serving, money-hungry types, and Lucas Brand was the most self-serving, money-hungry egomaniac of them all! She'd never been so frustrated by any one human being in her life. His was a debt of honor, for heaven's sake! And in the same breath that he slithered out of a loophole, he *dared* suggest his integrity had never been questioned? Well, she was questioning it now!

Suddenly, something inside her snapped, and a raw, primitive fury overwhelmed her, sending her storming to her feet. "When you made that promise to Mr. Roxbury, what was it? A sort of techno-bull token to get him off your back?"

Lucas's hawklike features grew wary, then hard, but the lid was off now, and she couldn't halt the words that flowed, angry and unguarded. "Just so we're clear, Mr. My-Integrity-Has-Never-Been-Questioned," she cried, stomping toward him. "I don't like to believe Mr. Roxbury made a mistake, but *I* think you're the *worst* choice in the world for Mr. Niceguy! What do you have to say to that?"

The patio took on the silence of the dead. Mortified by her unprofessional behavior, Jess could only stare

back as he watched her, his implacable expression unnerving.

The strained stillness was finally broken by a deep,
cynical chuckle. With more weariness than irritation
in his manner, he propped a lean hip on the railing.
"This may shock you, Mrs. Glen," he said, his dark eyes
glinting scornfully in the fading light. "But for once—
and probably for the only time in our dubious associ-
ation—we are in *perfect* agreement."

3

JESS SAW LUCAS BRAND sitting with two of his cronies in the plush restaurant, and her stomach lurched. She'd had two days to think about their last confrontation, and she vowed she wouldn't make the same mistakes again. Oh, she'd managed to get him to go along with the Mr. Niceguy plans, and he'd promised there would be no caterer, but he was still falling far short of the ideal.

So, here she was again—forced to prod him into shaping up. This time, she'd be smarter about it. This time, Mr. Roxbury would be her model. No matter how upset Lucas made her, she would pause and ask herself, *What would Norman do?* Her boss had such a graceful way of dealing with people, of handling them—why, it was Mr. Roxbury who'd gotten Lucas to agree to be Mr. Niceguy in the first place. Why hadn't she thought of using him as her model before? Kill the man with kindness. Be positive with a capital *P*. That was the ticket.

When the maître d' asked if Mr. Brand was expecting her, she smiled sweetly and lied, "Yes. Thank you."

Winding through the lunchtime crowd at one of Oklahoma City's poshest eateries, she prepped herself by thinking only happy thoughts. Positive visualizations of Lucas Brand reacting goodnaturedly to her gently worded requests. She also visualized calming things, like roses with dew on their petals, butterflies fluttering in a wildflower-strewn field, kittens curled up before a cozy fire. She inhaled deeply and exhaled slowly. "Butterflies, kittens, dew, roses . . ."

A nagging voice in her brain insisted on sneering, "No way, Jess. You aren't Mr. Roxbury. He'll get you flustered and angry and you're going to end up dumping ice water over his head."

She squelched the negative image, mumbling, "Butterflies, kittens, dew, roses, butterflies-kittens-dew-roses-butterflies-kittens-dew-roses." It became a thin-lipped, desperate mantra that marked her ever-slowing tread as she maneuvered toward his table.

When she was a few feet away, she realized the top executives of Virtual Vision Technology were in intense, though whispered, debate. Lucas was the only one not actually speaking. He wasn't quite lounging, for she doubted if the man ever relaxed. Sprawled elegantly, one elbow on the chair's arm, he was tapping a contemplative finger on his upper lip. His expression was critical, as though he wasn't happy with the bent of the discussion. As she neared, she heard a short, stubby fellow insist, "It can't be done, Lucas. Not in the time Takahashi's insisting on."

A redheaded man in his mid-thirties persisted, "It might be possible, if that receptor point problem—"

"Problem is putting it mildly!" the stubby man burst in over the redhead's remark. "Face it. We need too many receptor points. The infrared receiver can't distinguish between so many signals. Every time I quirk my little finger, the computer gives me a rude gesture."

"That'd be *my* first instinct," the redhead retorted. "You're such a fatalistic ass!"

"And you're a pigheaded fool! I told you both a month ago we couldn't go cordless, and—" The stubby man, his angry features ruddy all the way up to the top of his bald head, halted in midsentence, as he noticed Jess beside their table.

Then the redhead and Lucas glanced her way.

"Hello," the bald man said, struggling to stand. "May we help you?"

The redhead belatedly pushed up, too, his freckled features alight with male curiosity. Lucas merely sat there, looking dubious. "Mrs. Glen," he intoned, with mild surprise. "This is a coincidence."

She offered him a well-meant smile. "Your secretary told me where you were."

"I'll have to thank her for that," he muttered cynically.

She recognized his sarcasm, but struggled to ignore it. "May I have a word with you, Mr. Brand?" she asked, her tone as bright as she could manage.

He nodded, apparently suggesting that she speak her piece and go.

She felt a tremor of anxiety, wishing his disinterest didn't bother her so much. She mustn't allow him to upset her. After all, he was busy, and upset himself, considering what she'd just heard. Evidently things hadn't gotten much better with his big, important project since they'd last spoken. She reinforced her smile, prompting sweetly, "I'd prefer we were alone."

He gave her a speculative perusal, then with a curt nod, he indicated that his employees stay put. "You two try to keep from killing each other. I'll be right back."

"This may take more than a few minutes," she advised. "And let me say, I do so appreciate your generous offer to help."

As he rose from his chair, he gave her an unconvinced glance, but said nothing.

"Maybe you should tell them you'll meet them back at the office," she suggested, hoping repetition would reinforce the fact that he would not be returning soon.

His expression vaguely amused, he said, "They're not in the first grade, though they sometimes act like it. If they finish and I'm not back, they'll figure out what to do. Fletch and Sol are fairly bright for computer geniuses."

"Why, of course, you're right. You'll have to forgive me. I'm used to working with children and teenagers—"

"Mrs. Glen, I don't need to hear your résumé." Surprising her, he took her arm and guided her away. "Why don't we find a table and get on with it," he suggested, nodding to a waiter.

"Fine—fine," she murmured, oddly breathless. A nervous giggle escaped her throat, and she grimaced, hoping the restaurant noise was too loud for him to have heard. His grip was gentle, but firm, as he conducted her along. She clutched her briefcase with white-knuckled fingers, wanting the contact to end. The man's touch disturbed her.

Once they were seated, he sat back and crossed his arms, his posture one of weary dignity. He looked like a tired lion, reposing there. She swallowed, wishing he weren't quite so magnetic a man. Her wits seemed to do a little scattering around him. And her stupid giggle! Where had *that* come from?

"What is it?" he asked, finally.

Remember how Mr. Roxbury handles people, she told herself. When she faced him again, she was smiling. She noticed that he'd sat forward, loosely tenting his fingers on the tablecloth. That gave her an idea.

She'd read in her self-help book that if you lightly touched a person when talking to them, a psychological bond was formed, and the person being touched tended to be more agreeable. *Why not?* she decided. She was at a point where she was desperate to get this man to agree with her about anything—besides the fact that he was the world's worst choice for Mr. Niceguy.

Now that she thought about it, Mr. Roxbury patted people all the time. Must be something to it. Though she wasn't a "toucher" herself, and her family had never been much for hugging or holding hands, she sucked in a breath for courage, reached across the table, and determinedly patted his hands. "It's so nice to see you again, Mr. Brand," she enthused, feeling inept and out of her element. As believably as she could, she added, "I know it will be a pleasure working with you."

His glance shifted to her hand, then to her face. There was an odd mingling of mirth and irritation in his expression. She kept patting, feeling awkward, trying to work out her plan. She didn't want to accuse him of shirking his duty. Maybe if she acted like she assumed he'd just forgotten about—

"Why Lucas," a female voice declared from Jess's left. An attractive blonde of about Jess's age was sidling up to the table. She leaned down and pressed a kiss on his cheek. Lucas smiled coolly at the woman. She caressed his cheek fondly. "How are you? It's been, what—three months?"

Lucas started to rise, but the woman put a hand on his shoulder. "Please don't bother, I'm just passing by."

"It's nice to see you," Lucas said, with that same polished smile, but neither of the women was fooled into thinking he meant it. The blonde laughed and shook her head in a light rebuke.

"The name's Mary Anne. Mary Anne Brown, of the 'I'll-call-you-Mary-Anne' Browns." Glancing at Jess, the woman gave her a sympathetic nod. "You must be Lucas's, 'Miss November.' Enjoy it while it lasts." She ran her fingers through the hair at Lucas's nape, as though she couldn't help but touch him one last time. More to herself than to Jess, she murmured, "He has a demanding mistress."

After that veiled remark, she abruptly left. Jess felt embarrassed for the woman and couldn't think of anything to say. She stared absently at her water goblet.

"Mrs. Glen," Lucas said, cutting into her musings, "I never learned Morse code, so rather than tap out your message on my hands, why don't you just tell me why you're here."

Her gaze snapped to her fidgeting fingers, still curled over his. Mortified, she snatched them away and took a shaky sip of water in order to have a minute to compose herself.

Lucas cleared his throat, and she surreptitiously looked at him over the rim of her cut-crystal goblet.

His expression showed slight vexation, and she could see by the direction in which he was looking that he'd followed the blonde's exit.

She replaced her water glass on the table, feeling a twinge of pity for any woman who would get involved with this man. "I gather by 'demanding mistress,' she meant your work?"

He shifted back to look at her. "I don't know what the hell she meant. Can we get on with it?"

Neither of them spoke as coffee was served. When the waiter had gone, he ground out, "Okay, Mrs. Glen. So far in our relationship, you've played a neurotic Barbara Walters clone, a vacuum-cleaner salesman turned pit bull, and today you've done your impression of Miss Teenage America, whose talent is screwing up Morse code. It's been entertaining, but could we dispense with the games? Just give me your bottom line."

Fresh anxiety sliced through her, and she coughed nervously. He was in a foul mood, and wasn't going to take this well. Be that as it may, there was nothing left for her to do but take a deep breath and plunge in.

Reaching for her briefcase, she lifted it to the tabletop. "Okay, Mr. Brand." Snapping the fasteners open, she lifted the lid. "Bottom line." Pulling out a batch of rumpled papers, she held them in his direction. She was tired of trying to find ways to appease this man, and was glad he'd called her on her subterfuge. She simply wasn't cut out for deception. "As you can see, I have a problem."

His lips curved in a sardonic half smile. "I noticed. But I understand multiple-personality psychosis can be treated."

She frowned, then realized he'd made a small joke. Startled, she fixed her gaze on him. He had lowered his eyelids so that he could see out, but no one could see in. She resented his ability to do that. It was like trying to relate to a machine. "These are the essays I left for you to read when I was at your home the other night. If you'll remember, I said I'd need them by the day before Thanksgiving."

He picked them up and scanned them as the waiter served more coffee. "So?" he asked after a minute.

She stared, unbelieving. "So—*today* is the day before Thanksgiving. When I went by your home this morning to pick them up, assuming they'd be scored and evaluated, I found them exactly as I'd left them."

He was thumbing through the papers. "Some look like they've been chewed on."

"They may have been," she said, trying to remain calm. "Not all of them were written in the best possible atmosphere. A few may very well have been chewed, or worse. But that doesn't make the effort less worthy. Do you remember my telling you the ten winners would be announced at the Thanksgiving dinner? If you'll recall, their prize was a week at the Mr. Niceguy Retreat?" She pressed, "Is it coming back at all?"

He took a sip of his coffee, then admitted with a nod, "Right. It slipped my mind."

With blossoming hostility, Jess surveyed his unrepentant face. When she could bring herself to speak, she repeated, "It slipped your mind?" Her voice had lifted a tense octave, betraying her feelings.

There was a hardening of his features, though he retained a nonchalant half smile. "I told you I'm busy. You just witnessed how easily our project is falling into place. I have my two best men at each other's throats, I have *no* software and a nonresponse glove to offer my client—and only a couple of weeks to work out the bugs. I'm human. The damned essays slipped my mind. But I'll read them."

"When?" she prodded, with more than a hint of annoyance.

"When I have time," he retorted, his glance as stubborn as hers.

Mexican-standoff time. A dull throb started behind Jess's eyes as a gnawing sense of her inadequacy shrouded her—not for the first time in her life, either. All too often her parents had made the statement, "Jess, you'll never make anything of yourself if you can't be a leader! If you can't control people." She'd tried. But ultimately she always failed. And she was failing miserably today.

Just how competent did a person have to be to persuade someone to follow through on a debt of honor? Apparently, more competent than she. Defeated, she massaged her aching temples. "Mr. Brand," she began, "How do you feel about Norman Roxbury?" She peered up at him, hoping she wouldn't disgrace herself by bursting into tears. "How do you *really* feel? Off the record. I'd just like to know."

A troubled look stole across his face, then quickly disappeared. She waited in a silence that grew so aggressive it was cruel. Vaguely, she was aware of sounds around them—the clink of flatware against fine china, the rattle of a pastry cart, a tinkle of ice cubes, voices, the murmurs, and muted laughter of affluent patrons; even the faraway whine of a siren stretched across the tension-laden air to reach her ears. Around them the world marched on, but at their table, no movement existed; nothing was audible but the thundering of stark, expectant silence.

At length, Lucas started to speak, then looked away. When their eyes met again, his were angry, haunted.

Yet, in that harsh contact, Jess felt a stab of comprehension, and grasped his unspoken message across the distance. It was very simple and very painful. The truth of it distressed him, distressed him so much he couldn't admit it aloud. *He cared.* He didn't want to, but he did.

With a gritted oath, Lucas snatched up the essays and, to her astonishment, began to read.

She sat speechless for a few minutes. Surprised that he'd once again come through—if under extreme duress. She took a sip of coffee, gaping at him. Without realizing the degree of her concentration, she allowed her gaze to trail over his broad torso, which was sheathed in an expensive black suit, silk shirt and bold-patterned tie. His dark-eyed, sullen face was staggering in its appeal.

When she realized what an unhealthy direction her thoughts had taken, she pulled her lips between her teeth, biting hard, forcing her mind back to the problem at hand—the problem of trying to turn Lucas Brand into a willing Mr. Niceguy. Apparently her despondent sigh was audible, for he cast her an inquiring glance. She felt a shudder at the eye contact, and was dismayed to discover she was actually attracted to this guy.

How strange and unfair sexual desire could be. Her whole life plan, since her divorce, had been to steer clear of the type A male, and here she was stupidly going over the physical attributes of the most outrageously A-type male in the state of Oklahoma, like some smitten teenager.

What was worse, Lucas Brand was the very man who'd caused her a great deal of personal trauma over the past several years. There were few people in the world for whom she held more contempt. He had a cold, shrewd nature, and there was no room in the man's existence for flesh-and-blood relationships. Miss Mary Anne Brown had made that pitiably clear only moments ago. Jess knew she'd have to keep that in mind when her thoughts started to stray into fantasies involving Lucas's broad shoulders and sensual lips.

To keep her mind safely occupied, she ordered a salad, but managed to eat very little of it. All the time he said nothing, just frowned down at the pages as he read.

Once, their legs brushed, and Jess drew away, feeling a flush heat her cheeks. Lucas lifted his gaze briefly, but none of his thoughts registered on his guarded features.

About the time she gave up on being able to eat, the redheaded Fletch and the stocky Sol stopped by their table. Fletch cleared his throat to catch his boss's attention.

When Lucas looked up, Fletch said, "I think Sol came up with something. We're going to check it out."

Lucas pursed his lips, then nodded.

"You coming back to the office?" he added, casting a curious look at Jess.

"If I don't get hauled in for murder, first," Lucas muttered.

Tugging his collar, Fletch smiled uncertainly at the woman to whom he'd never been introduced, and headed toward the exit, trailed by Sol.

Startling Jess, Lucas thrust the pages at her. "Okay," he said impatiently. "I've marked the ten best."

She leafed through them. It appeared that he'd come to some solid conclusions. Reviewing her own notes, she found that they agreed on nine of the ten. She plucked out her choice along with his, and lifted them toward him. "Why Jack's over Barry's?"

His irritation at her continued intrusion into his life hung in the air between them like acrid smoke. He grabbed the two pages, scanning them both. "This kid's thankful his mother let him keep the stray dog he found. At least Barry's got a dog and a caring mother," he said, more to himself than to her. "This other boy, Jack, swears he can't find much to be thankful about. But he ends his essay with, 'I guess I'm thankful it doesn't cost to breathe.'"

Lucas looked at Jess. Along with the displeasure in his eyes, she saw something else. Something not quite readable. "There's anger in this boy's essay," he continued, "but underneath, there's humor, and a depth that goes beyond any of these other papers."

She saw his point but had to say, "He's so bitter. He's teetering on the edge of dropping out. A good seventy-five percent of these at-risk kids don't make it through high school, as it is. Jack looks like a really chancy case at best."

For a minute, Lucas didn't speak, and Jess watched as a muscle twitched in his jaw. There was a stamp of stubbornness there, in the thrust of his chin, and a boldness in his black eyes. Yet he didn't argue or snarl at her as she'd assumed he would; he merely shrugged. "You asked for my opinion, I gave it. My experience with troubled kids is—limited." He paused. For a second, no more, his face seemed bleak. Almost before she'd registered the expression, he was wearing that unreadable mask again.

Jess sensed he'd been speaking of himself, and her heart went out to him, which astonished her. Avoiding the brush of his fingers, she took the essays back. She wouldn't argue. It was a judgment call, and, he, after all, was Mr. Niceguy—at least for the next week.

"Okay, though I'm not sure I agree. It's Jack," she acknowledged without inflection. Stacking the pages, she deposited them in her briefcase before facing him again. When she did, his inspection of her seemed disapproving.

"What?" she asked, fairly sure what he had on his mind.

"You already read them."

She nodded. "I'm your assistant. I'm helping you, remember?"

His brief, twisted grin was humorless. "Mrs. Glen, you're going to have to look up that word. For your information, it doesn't mean *jerk around*."

"I'm sorry if you feel that way," she retorted. Standing, she brushed at her slim suit skirt. "As you've repeatedly informed me, you're a busy man. I won't keep you any longer."

He watched her rise, but said nothing.

"I'll see you first thing in the morning." She picked up her briefcase and faced him, trying to look pleasant. It was hard. Her nerves were in shreds.

"What, exactly, is 'first thing' to you?" he asked.

"I'll be there at eight sharp, with volunteers to help get the place ready. The kids will arrive at ten."

He nodded, then stood towering over her. "I'll schedule my meeting for six and try to be back."

Her eyes widened, and she felt a new prick of annoyance. Through a tired sigh, she said, "You just won't give this one-hundred percent, will you?"

His gaze bore into hers for a long moment. Finally, and in a tone courteous but grim, he warned her, "Bottom line, Mrs. Glen—I can't."

THANKSGIVING MORNING, a truck arrived at the Brand residence with six big turkeys, a pile of pumpkins, boxes and bags of assorted vegetables, dry goods and utensils.

Instantly and with all the vivid fireworks of an erupting volcano, Lucas's cook came down with a migraine headache that would have made Camille look like a happy little homemaker. Though Jess tried to assure her that the turkeys would be cooked outside on charcoal grills that had been delivered for that purpose, the thin, nasal woman flailed theatrically, then fumed off into the bowels of the house.

Jess hadn't seen Lucas, but knew he must have made it back from his meeting. In the distance she heard the cook wailing that she was condemned along with the rest of his staff to endure "The Thanksgiving Dinner from Hell."

Jess and her volunteers began moving sawhorses and planks into the large garage, emptied of luxury cars for the occasion by a good-natured chauffeur. Minutes later, she saw the cook barreling through the activity, packed suitcases clenched in both hands. It was clear that she was having nothing to do with the Thanksgiving invasion, and had thrown a fit and quit.

Uh-ohhh, Jess thought. This would be another thorn in Lucas's side. She could see him now, somewhere in his vast house, cursing them for frightening away an employee. She wondered if any other members of his staff were packing up in a huff.

Around nine, as she was spreading paper table-cloths over the makeshift counters, in the garage, she spied Lucas. His tall, broad-shouldered form loomed in the door that led from the garage into the house—Mr. Buttoned-down himself, in a beige suede sport coat, classic gray trousers, silk tie and handsewn loafers. Not exactly dressed to spend a day scraping pumpkins and playing touch football. She exhaled despondently. What had she expected? Actual cooperation?

With a twinge of anxiety, she realized his somewhat judgmental scrutiny was focused on her. When their eyes met, she grew flustered. She was clad in jeans and a heavy, red wool sweater. Suddenly, a surge of old in-securities rushed through her, for she'd been brought up in a home where jeans were considered low-class at-tire.

Her parents had contended that the wearing of jeans was tantamount to a mortal sin. While her folks had had private prep-school sensibilities, they could ill af-ford it. So she'd had to endure attending public school while adhering to her parents' dress code.

Each time there'd been a casual party thrown by one of her classmates, and she was the only one to show up in ruffles and ribbons, she'd been humiliated. She still cringed at the memories. Too many times she'd been driven to tears, begging her parents to reconsider. But no. "First impressions, Jessica," her mother had preached time and again. "Never, *never* allow your first impression to be less than the best! Jeans give the wrong sort of image for a Ritter. Image is everything!"

Well, maybe to her mother and father, jeans were for lower-class types, but to her, ribbons and ruffles had made her the object of childish ridicule, and utterly, abjectly lonely. Nowadays, she only "dressed for success" when Mr. Roxbury's needs required such clothing. She was most comfortable in jeans, helping troubled kids—and most uncomfortable in suits, rubbing elbows with self-important specimens like Lucas Brand.

The man studying her from beneath lowered lids would have been her parents' ideal son. However, he was far from *her* ideal!

The unease she always felt around him—an unease she feared to put a name to—had returned with a vengeance. No matter how much she wanted to dart off and lose herself in the confusion of laughing, scrambling volunteers, she did need to speak with him. It was part of her job. The kids would be arriving in less than an hour, and there was no putting it off. Her adrenaline level shot up to prepare her for conflict as Jess propelled herself in his direction.

He made her come all the way to him. Didn't even move down the three steps to the garage level. Her unease swelled. It was clear that he didn't plan to make her job easier by giving an inch. Trying to discipline her voice to maintain the facade of nonchalance, she said, "Good morning, Mr. Brand. I hope we're not inconveniencing you too much."

His rough-hewn features were arresting, even in disapproval. "Don't think a thing about it, Mrs. Glen," he said flatly. "My house and my staff—what's left of it—are at your disposal."

She heard the mockery, but chose to ignore it. "Thanks. As you see, we'll be having the kids do most of the work here in the garage to spare your house."

"I'm gratified."

"And though we're cooking the turkeys outside, we'll need the kitchen—"

"Mrs. Glen," he interrupted, making her lose her train of thought.

"Yes?" she asked, apprehensive and not sure why.

"Where's *Mr.* Glen? Is he here?"

She flinched at the unexpected question. With watchful hesitation, she tried to formulate an answer. Nothing came. Nothing smart, or casual or flip. Only the plain truth, so she simply stated it. "I—he—we're divorced." Divorce wasn't against the law, for heaven's sake, so she didn't know why the admission bothered her so. Or did she? She glanced at him with a sideways squint. His face registered nothing in particular, no great joy or disgust. She wanted to change the subject, so she asked, "Do you own any jeans?"

He lifted a brow. "Why?"

"Because you'll ruin those clothes. Don't you have any casual things?"

He pursed his lips, seeming to be in sober contemplation. "Whose idea was it?" he asked after a pause.

"About wearing jeans?"

"The divorce. Whose idea?"

Her cheeks blazed. "I hope you don't take this badly," she blurted, tasting bitter bile. "But that question was uncalled-for, and positively none of your business!"

He moved to lounge against the doorjamb, sizing her up with a one-sided grin. "How, exactly, would you have phrased it if you *had* wanted me to take it badly, Jess? I hope you don't mind me calling you Jess."

"To be frank," she muttered, "I'd prefer it if you had to call me *long-distance*."

He shook his head and chuckled at her. "You don't have to be defensive about being divorced. It's a big club."

"That's easy for you to say," she retorted, wishing she *weren't* defensive—or at least that it didn't show so much. But when Bill had walked out on her, it had only served to reinforce her feelings of failure, as well as her aversion for the selfishly upwardly mobile. "What would you know about it, anyway?" she challenged.

"A little." He smiled without humor, a rather melancholy effort. "I've been a card-carrying member of the club for fifteen years."

She blinked, startled. She'd never heard that he'd been married. "Oh—I—I— You must have married young..." she stuttered.

He shrugged his hands into his pants pockets, glancing away. "I'll check with my chauffeur."

She squinted at him, baffled. "You have to ask your chauffeur if you married young?"

His brilliant black eyes fixed on her for a split second before he turned away. "Hardly," he muttered. "But my chauffeur's been known to wear jeans. Maybe I could borrow a pair."

4

LUCAS SAT BENEATH AN autumn-flushed oak on the grassy bank of the lake. The mouthwatering aroma of charcoaled turkey mingled with the crisp tang of the late-November afternoon. Kids wearing bright parkas were scattered about the grounds in bunches, like fallen leaves. Giggling groups lounged at the water's edge laughing and joking on blankets as they finished the dinner they'd helped prepare.

Sitting alone, Lucas viewed the noisy turmoil with bitter melancholy. As far as work went, the day had been an utter waste. Fletch and Sol were at the office, and had called him a half dozen times to confer. Jess had eyed him darkly each time he'd grabbed up his portable phone to discuss the latest Takahashi problem.

If that hadn't been enough, memories of the Mr. Niceguy Thanksgiving Dinner he'd attended long ago resurfaced to plague him. It was a part of his life he'd tried to forget, but Mr. Roxbury and his bothersome assistant were dredging it up again, and remembering was painful.

Both as a boy and a young man, he'd felt deeply—maybe too deeply for his own good. He'd suffered several traumatic losses—first his parents, then his grandmother and finally his wife. Over the past fifteen years he'd programmed himself, like one of his computers, to feel nothing, to need no one, and he didn't like this tug of long-buried emotions he was feeling today.

A shout drew his attention to the makeshift game of touch football that was going on not far away. Jess was playing quarterback, and not for the first time that day, he eyed her thoughtfully. She seemed more secure than he'd ever seen her, obviously in her element with the kids. She was also the worst quarterback he'd ever seen. Strange. The boys and girls on her team didn't seem to mind her fumbles and wild throws. They laughed, having a good time, even knowing they were losing.

Lucas had never been able to abide losing. Not even a simple game. He watched her fumble another toss, feeling an odd envy for people who could let themselves go the way she did around these kids. He couldn't recall the last time he'd relaxed and laughed out loud. Over the years, he'd trained himself to be self-contained, and to concentrate on work, and he was proud of his rationality and sense of purpose.

He supposed he was too much like the ant and not enough like the grasshopper for some people's tastes. Mrs. Jess Glen's, for instance. He grunted with resentment. Who was she to find fault, being the world's worst football player?

Glancing around, he spotted Jack, the boy whose essay he'd chosen as the best. The teenager was slouched under another oak not far away, his features glum. He'd acted exactly like Jack at that long-ago Thanksgiving dinner—aloof and unfriendly, feeling out of place and angry, with no control over his life.

His grandmother had been dead two years when he'd come to the Mr. Niceguy dinner. Grandma Jane had been the only stability he could remember in his young life, his parents having deserted him when he was five. After his grandmother's death, he'd been shuffled around from one dismal foster home to another, where nobody cared if he stayed or ran away. So, he invariably ran.

He hadn't known why he'd bothered to write his essay that day so long ago. Maybe deep inside him there'd been a dim glimmer of hope that things could get better. He'd figured out that nobody was going to do anything for him. So, if he was ever to have anything, he'd need to take control of his world and keep a stranglehold on it. Fearing that it might be his last chance, he'd written the thing, pouring his heart and his anger onto those pages.

Glancing back at Jack, Lucas recalled when Mr. Roxbury had walked up to the tree under which he'd been sitting that day, very much the way Jack was today—glowering, cursing everybody and everything. Roxbury had sat down and offered Lucas a cup of hot cocoa, saying, "You wrote the best essay of the bunch, my boy. I have a feeling there won't be any stopping you in this world."

Lucas winced at the memory. His fingers were laced together, his elbows resting on his knees. He stared at his hands for a long, pensive moment. Why was he thinking about that damned cocoa, now?

He recalled what he'd thought when Norman had brought the cup to him, and he'd caught a whiff of it. He hadn't had cocoa since before his grandmother's death. The familiar smell had wrenched at his heart. Upset, he'd sneered at the idea of accepting a cup of hot cocoa—mumbled something about it being for sissies and babies. Acting tough, he'd turned his back, too angry, hurt and mistrustful to be civil.

Still, at that moment, Lucas's life had changed. He'd sensed it even then. Lucas had a feeling Roxbury had known it, too, for as he rose to leave, he'd touched Lucas's shoulder. "You've been in a dark cage, my boy," he'd said. "I'm handing you a key, because you've got the brains and the nerve to unlock that iron door." He'd patted again, encouraging, "I'll be proud to watch when you step into the sunshine."

Eyes narrowed, Lucas studied Jack. He looked closed, resentful, sullen. If Norman were here, that kid would be facing a steaming cup of cocoa right now, along with a gentle smile and a pat on the shoulder. After all, Jack's *was* the best essay. The boy didn't know it yet, but he was going to win one of the ten coveted spots on the retreat and, what was probably even more reward as far as the kids were concerned, get to miss a week of school.

Lucas knew he should go over there to say something positive to the boy. But, hell, he wasn't Norman. What could he say that wouldn't sound fake and forced? *Hey, kid, you wrote a good essay. You've got a shot at not becoming an ax murderer. Have some cocoa....*

He closed his eyes. It sounded stupid, even to him. What would a street-smart, nineties-style, borderline juvenile-delinquent do with cocoa?

But that kid was his responsibility, today. For all it was worth, he was Mr. Niceguy. Maybe he ought to—

His cellular phone trilled and he jerked it from his jeans hip pocket. *Saved by the bell.* Flipping it open, he barked, "Brand, here." His jaw clenched. Sol was off

on another whining, it-can't-be-done tangent. Lucas
cut in impatiently, "Sol, we don't have time for negative crap. Try this. *KW* equals *VR*-to-the-fourth-power
minus *S*—" He was interrupted when Sol misunderstood what he'd said. "No, not *F. S* as in—" Something
thumped solidly against his boot. He heard a shriek and
felt someone land like an explosion of TNT in his lap.
The agony of being hit hard in his groin was so intense,
he barely noticed as a football glanced off his forehead
and wobbled away along the ground.

"*Shit!*" he ground out, pain shooting through his
body like red-hot buckshot, transforming him into a
bent-over cripple. Though the phone was no longer at
his ear, he could hear Sol's startled inquiry. Lucas
brought the phone back up, rasping through clenched
teeth, "Yes, *S* as in *shit*. I'll call you back." He clicked
off and dropped the phone to the dry grass, hoping for
a quick death.

The human missile that had caused his injury was
righting herself. A part of his brain that was still min-
imally functioning registered that it was Jess Glen. She
groaned, squinted around, then seemed to realize who
and what had broken her fall. Her cheeks, already
pinkened from the game, quickly darkened to a flam-
ing cherry when she noticed she was cradled in Lucas's
lap. Sliding to the grass, she mumbled, "Oh, I—I'm
sorry. I was going after a long one."

Her flinch told Lucas she knew her remark had come
out sounding lewd, considering the part of his anatomy she'd collided with. She stuttered on, "Ball—that
is . . ." She bit her lip. "I meant, *foot*—"

Because speech was difficult for him at the moment, he clutched her arm to stop her babbling. It worked. She went immediately mute, her eyes wide and fretful.

"Forget it," he finally managed, hoarsely. "I'd planned on having myself gelded for Christmas, anyway."

Her concerned expression eased slightly at his quip. "Are you—going to be okay? Should I call a doctor. Maybe get some ice?"

"Hell," he muttered, wishing she'd get off it. "Have you ever seen a man with an ice pack on his . . ." He let the remark die, jerking his head toward the youngsters who'd gathered around. "Drop it before they start calling me Mr. Nice-Eunuch."

"You sure?" she asked, hesitant, but a faint light had begun to twinkle in her eyes. "I could help you to the house, or something."

"I said, *drop it*." He released her shoulder. "Men don't die from this. Now, go."

She started to stand, then turned back, lips twitching. "This probably isn't the best time, but we need to start gathering the kids for the awards ceremony." Strangled laughter bubbled in her throat and she cleared it, straightening her face. "I'm sorry."

"You must love a good plane crash."

"Forgive me, but your 'Mr. Nice-Eunuch' remark struck me funny."

He continued to frown at her, but his rancor had dissipated. That puzzled him, considering his lower gut felt as if it had been slammed by a wrecking ball. "Pain brings out the Jerry Seinfeld in me, I guess."

She sat back, and with a tentative half grin, suggested, "Maybe you should be in pain more often."

"I expect you'll see to that."

"All in the spirit of giving." Her expression softened into an actual smile, unforced, even slightly friendly. "When do you think you'll be able to—er—be mobile?"

"Give me five minutes."

Nodding, she pushed up to stand.

As she walked away, Lucas let out a heavy breath, waiting out the throbbing in his groin. He decided that for all her pushy, puritanical faults, Jess Glen had a fair bedside manner. Too bad she had that liberal, bleeding-heart mentality—the type that lived for a good cause. She probably ran her life flying off on one emotional tangent or another, a bundle of feelings refusing to be reasoned with.

People probably couldn't be significant in her life unless they were needy or in pain. She'd only really smiled at him when he'd been hurt. Leaning back against the rough tree bark, he found himself reflecting idly that any man who got Mrs. Heart-On-Her-Sleeve Jess Glen into bed no doubt had to bash himself in the head with a tire iron and lapse into unconsciousness, first. Lucas chuckled at his train of thought. What did he care what turned that woman on?

After a minute or two, he noticed Jack, still sitting under the tree. The boy was staring at Lucas and smirking. The way to that damned kid's funny bone was through debilitating injury, it appeared. As the stinging in his gut ebbed, Lucas muttered under his breath, "Keep it up, little Mr. Marquis de Sade, and you'll get force-fed a mug of cocoa."

THE SUN WAS SETTING and the evening had brought with it a brisk north wind, so it was decided the announcement of the essay winners should be held inside. The kids were ushered into Lucas's great room. While that was going on, the band of volunteers, Mr. Niceguy recipients of years past, or spouses of recipients, were whisking the kitchen and garage clean.

Jess and Lucas, being in charge of the awards, were inside with the kids. The stand-in Mr. Niceguy stood before the window-wall, talking on his cellular phone. Behind him, the glowing sky tinted the room's white walls and ceiling a soft magenta. The kids, in awe of both the opulence of the house and the grandeur of the sunset, had grown quiet.

Jess helped usher stragglers to empty spots on the carpet—even Lucas's huge living room, containing two eight-foot couches, twelve dining chairs, a wide brick hearth and various other scattered seating arrangements, couldn't accommodate forty-three fourteen-year-olds.

As she was trying to coax Jack out of his sullen stance near the kitchen door, Jess risked a glance at her host, clad in faded stone-washed denims. He was finally off the phone, and was leaning against one of the glass-paned doors that led to the terrace.

Shed of attire more suited to his high-powered business persona, Lucas exuded a virility that was hard to ignore. She knew exactly *how* hard, for she'd been working at it all day. Scanning those close-fitting jeans, Jess was highly suspicious that they'd ever belonged to the chauffeur. The way they molded to Lucas's hips and thighs was obscene. The chauffeur was scrawnier,

bonier. He could never have faded those stress points
in such a shamelessly *sexy* way.

Against her better judgment, she continued to pe-
ruse Lucas. He was wearing scuffed, black cowboy
boots and a heavy gray turtleneck that accentuated his
dark good-looks. She sighed. What a shame such a
wickedly handsome exterior was wasted on this cold-
blooded man. She reluctantly admitted that he didn't
look the slightest bit cold-blooded, right now. Neither
did he look like a computer genius who spent his days
crouched over microscopic chips and wires. No. This
minute, Lucas Brand held all the allure of an Oklahoma broncobuster—a bold cowboy who lived and
loved by the seat of his pants, not a coldly calculating
executive whose only passions were raw data printouts and stock-market reports.

It was funny how clothes could transform a person.
She found herself hoping those really were his jeans,
and that every so often he let himself be recklessly human. He'd certainly confirmed he was human, at least
as far as being capable of feeling physical pain. Why,
he'd almost been *vulnerable*, and for a few crazy seconds she'd actually liked the guy.

Her cheeks burned from the memory of crashing into
his lap. She bit her lip, guiltily recalling the pleasant
hardness of his thighs, the mellow scent of his breath
against her cheek and—

Lucas shifted his glance, catching her in the act of
studying him. She swallowed, spinning away. "Come
on, Jack," she coaxed, oddly breathless. "There's a spot
up front, next to the coffee table."

He screwed up his mouth in a frown. "Naw."

"Oh, for pity's sake," she rebuked with a weak laugh and a shake of her head. "Give a girl a break, will ya?" She took his hand and tugged. "If anybody bites you, I'll sock 'em. Okay?"

He looked her up and down, clearly doubtful that she could do much protecting. "You and who else?" he asked, sounding bored.

"Me and that big dude in the turtleneck sweater." It surprised her that she was giving Lucas any credit for being interested in the well-being of these kids—a man who cared squat about anything but money.

"I don't think he likes me much," Jack bellyached, eyeing Lucas with uncertainty.

She tugged the boy along. "Are you kidding? He's crazier about you than I am." That was the truth. Jess doubted Jack's ability to stick with high school, his attitude being so sulky, but Lucas's decision was final. "Come on. Let's get this show on the road."

Once all the kids were seated, she joined their host at the front of the room. "You want to do this?" she asked him in a low aside.

With narrowed eyes, he said, "Take a wild guess."

She smiled up at him for the benefit of their audience, making sure he could read the irritation in her glance. "You make an effort, just once, and I'll have a heart attack and die."

He grinned down at her, his brief flash of teeth striking and irreverent. "A tempting offer," he drawled. "I'll keep it in mind."

Clearing her throat with dire meaning, she turned around to face the boys and girls. Holding up both hands, she signaled for quiet to the few who were still rustling and wriggling. "Okay, folks," she began, "it's time to announce the essay-contest winners who'll come back here tomorrow and spend a week at Mr. Niceguy's Thanksgiving Retreat."

There was renewed buzzing among the teenagers, so Jess waved them quiet again. "As you know, there are a fixed number of slots for the retreat, so we were limited to picking ten essays. But as far as Mr. Niceguy and I are concerned, you're all winners."

She'd had a hard time saying "Mr. Niceguy" without making a face. Lucas Brand had proven to be *no* shining model for the term, but she struggled on: "Every essay was well thought-out and worthy of a prize. And as you know, even if you don't win today, you're *all* still eligible for Mr. Niceguy college scholarships, as long as you finish school and your grades qualify you for college acceptance. Or you can choose a technical school if you prefer."

She didn't go into the reasons why these particular young people qualified. All of them were aware of their situations—children of poverty-level single-parent families, or wards of the court in foster care. "At Risk" kids, they were labeled, because statistics indicated that kids in those circumstances were most at risk of dropping out of school and getting involved in drugs and crime.

Sadly, even with the Mr. Niceguy incentives, at least half of these boys and girls would eventually drop out; only a handful would go on to receive Mr. Niceguy scholarships. Nevertheless, it was Jess's belief that each year, Mr. Roxbury's efforts did save young lives, did turn them away from the ravages of ignorance and crime. That belief was what kept those dedicated to the Mr. Niceguy program going.

Omitting any reference to the negative, she smiled and forged on, "Remember, even if you decide college isn't for you, if you make it through high school with at least a C-plus grade average, the Mr. Niceguy program will give you two thousand dollars as a reward for your success."

The kids made appreciative sounds, and she had to hush them again. Two thousand dollars sounded like a fortune to a fourteen-year-old. It was meant to. Money was one of the few things these kids responded to, since money—or the lack of it—dominated their lives, and in all too many cases lured them astray.

She raised her voice to be heard over the low buzzing. "The Mr. Niceguy program is here to compensate you for your hard work and to help you complete your education. And we'd be more than happy to hand out checks on graduation day to every one of you sitting here tonight."

She scanned the watchful faces, wishing every child there could come to the retreat, hating to disappoint any of them. Every child here was exceptional in Jess's mind. The Mr. Niceguy program, with the help of area schools, had sent out hundreds of flyers about the contest to eligible students. These forty-three had responded. They wanted a better life, and they'd made an effort. She breathed a silent prayer that they would all succeed, despite the odds against them.

Clearing a lump that had formed in her throat, she said, "Enough lecturing. Let's get on to the list of winners." Shifting, she thrust a sheet of paper into Lucas's hand, eyed him threateningly and declared in a loud, firm tone, "Mr. Niceguy will announce the winners."

Annoyance flickered across Lucas's face, then he composed himself behind a casual mask. "Thank you, Mrs. Glen," he intoned, without a hint of the menace Jess knew he harbored because of her dirty trick. "And Happy Thanksgiving to you, too."

She cast him a sidelong glare and caught his devilish grin. He was plotting revenge, the bum. Still, a thrill raced through her at the sight of that crooked, seductive mouth.

"All right, ladies and gentlemen," he began, scanning his list. "Here are the condemned ten." He paused to survey the confused faces. "I say condemned, because I understand you'll be eating your own cooking, and I've *tasted* it."

There was a burst of laughter, and Jess found herself staring at him. A joke? Evidently he'd made a few after-dinner speeches in his time. As the giggling died down, Jess wondered why Lucas had made any effort to put the kids at ease. Probably force of habit from years of speech-making.

He began to read, and after each name there was a burst of applause. Jack's last name was Zeeman, so he'd be the final winner announced. Jess found herself growing eager to see his expression, and was glad now that Lucas had insisted on selecting Jack. Maybe this endorsement would be the turning point he needed in his life.

When Jack's name was called, no pleasant emotion registered on his face. Not even surprise. His frown merely deepened. Jess called for quiet, because the room had broken up into animated conversations, as well as squeals and hugs from girls who'd discovered that a favorite friend had also been chosen.

Of course, there were downcast faces. She felt the usual pang about that, but clapped her hands for quiet. "Okay, gang, we've got a surprise gift for you all in the kitchen." She gestured in that direction, reminding, "The bus will be here in a few minutes. Enjoy your gift and *Happy Thanksgiving,* everybody!"

The kids were trailing out where their parting gifts were waiting, the brightly wrapped tokens a ploy for the losers to take their minds off their loss. And besides cupcakes and a pen set, there was a final note to remind them that they were all still in the running for scholarships. Jess looked around. Jack hadn't moved from his spot on the floor. She went over to him and squatted down. "Hey, congratulations." She affectionately squeezed a fisted hand. "Are you surprised?"

He avoided looking at her by averting his face. With the force of a blow, it occurred to Jess that Jack was fighting back tears. The poor kid. Never in his wildest dreams, had he expected this. She felt her eyes well up, and unable to form words without sounding quivery, she could only squeeze his hand in understanding.

Not wanting to embarrass him further, she stood and turned away, only to bump into Lucas's chest. He stepped back and started to speak, then saw her brimming eyes, and frowned in confusion. Overwhelmed by her emotions, Jess was unable to explain. Instead, she touched his chest fondly in mute apology. He'd been right to choose Jack. She knew that now.

Lucas had been the intuitive one, not she; but instead of being upset or jealous at his perceptiveness, she was elated—for Jack's sake. She hadn't suspected Lucas had such sensitivity in him. He certainly hid it well.

Briefly, Jess met Lucas's confused glance, tried again to express her feelings, but without success. Brushing away a stray tear, she shook her head and rushed off toward the kitchen.

5

THE TEENAGERS WERE GONE, and Lucas's house was as quiet as an abandoned warehouse. The only sound was the brittle thump of branches tossed about by the night wind as they crashed against the eaves. The noises were unsettling, and Jess felt very alone.

She waited in the kitchen for Lucas, who'd disappeared fifteen minutes before. There was no doubt in her mind that he was on the phone—again—and she found herself thrumming her nails on the kitchen table. Hating that nervous habit, she drew her hands into her lap and fisted them, then looked absently around. The kitchen was large and L-shaped, stark white, with gray accents here and there. She was seated at a round smoked-glass table located in the short leg of the L. There was a fireplace nearby—brick, but painted unobtrusively white.

The floor was made of polished squares of silvery granite. Not a scratch, not a speck of dirt, was to be seen anywhere on its surface. Like the rest of his house, Lucas's kitchen was as clean as a hound's tooth—trim, neat and spare.

There were no baseboards, no architectural excesses. All edges seemed to come together as sharp as knives. His was a world without clutter or sentiment. Admittedly, it was aesthetically pleasing, in a restrained way. She once again thought of this place as an extension of Lucas Brand, himself. He was certainly aesthetically pleasuring—in a restrained way. She bit her lip, not pleased that she was dwelling on the man in *any* way.

But her mind, drifting against her will, recalled a while ago when Jack had been close to tears, and how she'd glanced back at him on her retreat to the kitchen. She'd stumbled to a halt when she saw Lucas actually hunkering down beside the boy, speaking to him. She'd give a month's salary to know what he'd said.

A few minutes later, Jack had joined the others in the kitchen to get his parting gift. He looked solemn, showing no trace of emotion. He hadn't even turned Jess's way. Whatever Lucas had said, it hadn't changed the boy, much. Well, she mused, not even Mr. Roxbury performed instant miracles.

Hearing a sound, Jess knew Lucas was finally making an appearance. Stiffening, she turned. "I thought you'd flown to the Bahamas or . . ." she began, aiming to keep the mood light. Then she noticed that he'd changed clothes. He wore brown dress slacks, a button-down ecru shirt and a tie with splashes of earth tones, and as he walked, he was pulling on a tan sport coat.

Once again he'd donned that sophisticated veneer that was both annoying and intimidating. The unexpected change startled her, and she blurted out, "Do you have a date?" Her question sounded accusatory, and she winced. She hadn't meant it that way. Of course, he could have a date if it pleased him.

He strolled toward to her, his dress shoes making a crisp clicking sound on the granite floor. "Do I have a what?" he asked.

As he passed to take a seat on the opposite side of the table, his scent surrounded her. She inhaled the clean, freshly showered smell, noting a hint of after-shave that reminded her of cedar and leather. With a tight smile, she thought quickly. "Uh—I was just wondering if I could have some coffee?"

He'd pulled out a chair, then stopped, scanning the kitchen counter nearby. "Looks like there's some left." He started in that direction, but she fairly leaped up. "*No*—don't bother. I can do it." She wasn't sure why, but she couldn't allow this man to serve her. Maybe she didn't care to be obliged to him in even a small way. The less involved they were outside strict business dealings, the better.

As she scrambled from her seat, he flicked his wrist up to look at his watch. "Whatever," he mumbled. "Can we make this quick? I have a meeting at my office in thirty minutes."

She halted, her lips open, ready to demand, *You have a meeting, tonight?* But she stopped, the inquiry dying on her tongue. He'd sat down and was pinching the bridge of his nose as though he had a headache. She felt a rush of sympathy for him. If he'd had a meeting at six this morning, and had another one at seven this evening, he was putting in very long days. Instead of making her planned sharp remark, she went over to the coffeemaker and asked, "Would you like a cup?"

He glanced at her, his brows lifting in surprise. "If you don't mind."

"How about a couple of aspirin?"

"I'd kill for some," he admitted quietly.

With trembly hands, she poured two mugs of coffee and returned to the table. From her purse she drew out a tin of aspirin, lifted the lid and held the container toward him. "No improvement with your program?" she asked, surprised that she was actually concerned.

"Not much." He tipped back his head and downed the headache remedy without benefit of liquid.

She took a sip of coffee—it was strong, but revitalizing after the nerve-racking day—and murmured against the cup's rim, "I'm sorry to hear that."

He'd raised his mug halfway to his lips. "Sorry enough to give me a reprieve until spring?"

Her mood lurched from nervousness to dejection. "I'm not your jailer," she said. "You know you can quit any time."

Avoiding his face, she added, "You probably ought to know, Mr. Roxbury had another stroke last night."

She heard Lucas's raw curse and couldn't help but peer at his expression. His features had darkened. "How bad?" he asked.

She shrugged. "Thankfully, not as bad as it could have been, but it set back his physical therapy."

Lucas glared at his watch, then in a harsh voice, demanded, "What did you need to see me about? I can be five minutes late."

She inhaled, feeling both grudging and grateful. Lucas's concern for Mr. Roxbury had won out again—barely. *Why does it have to take a man practically on his deathbed to get your attention!* her mind raged, but she hid her feelings. Holding fast to her temper, she opened her briefcase and pulled out a typed list. "Okay, we don't have to discuss all of this. I saw stables and what looked like a bunkhouse a ways back from the house. Do you have horses on the property?"

Again, his coffee cup halted halfway to his lips. "Horses? What would I do with horses? I don't have time to drive a car, let alone ride a horse."

She ignored the gibe with effort, jotting a note. "We'll have to rent some for horseback riding. I'll handle it, but you have to okay the funds, since you'll be paying for them." He took a swallow of coffee as she asked, "What about a hay wagon?"

"What about one?"

She peered up from her list. "Do you *have* one?"

"Did you see one in the garage?"

Trying to hide the sting his mockery caused, she made another note. "We'll have to rent one of those, too."

"What the hell for?" He sounded tired.

"The hayride. That'll be the next-to-last day." She tapped the pen against her upper lip. "What have I forgotten?"

"The stagecoach?" he suggested wearily. "Maybe five thousand longhorns for the cattle drive to Abilene?"

Without comment, she deposited her list in her briefcase, refusing to take the bait. "I'll tend to the horse and wagon rentals first thing in the morning. I just needed your authorization." Closing her case, she faced him, struggling to retain a pleasant, professional facade. "The kids and I and four volunteers will be here at ten."

He took another swallow of his coffee. "Are we finished?"

She nodded. Then, recalling the vision of Lucas hunched down, talking to Jack in the living room, she had to add, "Just one thing."

He'd started to stand, anticipating the end of the meeting, but sat back down, his expression forbidding. "Make it quick."

She was antsy about asking, and couldn't figure out why. Apparently some part of her wanted to think there was more to him that was human than his ability to feel physical pain. She'd seen a flash of something entirely charming when she'd embarrassed him out there on the lawn. Charming and unguarded, and worthwhile. He hadn't quite smiled at her; still, she'd had the oddest feeling he'd wanted to, but had forced himself to remain stern. She'd felt it again when she'd seen him bend down to talk to Jack. She *hoped* she had, anyway....

Something warm and strong closed about her hand, and her glance fell to see long, male fingers covering hers. Her eyes widening with surprise, she stared up at him questioningly.

"Let me guess," he said. "Either the British are coming or you're sinking hard by the bow."

"What?" she whispered. His fingers squeezing hers seemed to have scattered her wits.

He nodded toward her hand, still covered by his. "Your Morse code." His penetrating eyes were on her, and his grimness seemed to have thawed slightly. "Jess," he began. "Is it me, all men, or all adults who make you nervous?"

The room had grown warm. Hot, even. Her brain gave her hand strict instructions about removing itself from his, but nothing happened; her hand remained lightly captured, with no urge to be free.

With monumental effort, she hurriedly withdrew her hand and declared, "Don't be silly. Why should I be afraid of you?" It sounded more convincing than she'd dared hope.

"I—I was just curious about something, and I wasn't sure it was my business to ask." That was true, but not as true as it might have been if she'd told him everything. About her fear of type *A*s, for instance. But what was worse, was a truth she dared not even think about—how his sultry glance bothered her when he stared at her just so, or how his touch . . .

She swallowed, deciding it would be best not to dwell on that. "I—I was wondering what you said to Jack earlier. When he was sitting on the floor in your living room."

Lucas's brows came together, as though the question had come out of left field and wasn't one he wanted to answer. "What I said?" He shrugged, looking impatient. "I don't recall."

She prodded, "When you squatted down beside him."

His lids slipped down over his eyes, masking his thoughts. "I imagine you mean when I asked if he was okay."

She felt a torrent of relief. *How nice.* "Yes, he was really overwhelmed about winning, wasn't he? It was sweet of you to say something."

"Sweet?" There was contempt in his tone.

She nodded, her smile faltering. "Of course. You noticed he was near tears and you cared enough to check on him. I think that's sweet."

He sat forward, placing his hands flat on the table. The move seemed vaguely ominous. "Damn it to hell," he ground out. "Look, my little bleeding heart. Don't make assumptions about me based on your Pollyanna view of the world. I wasn't being *sweet*. I stepped on the kid's hand, and I checked to make sure I hadn't broken it." He pushed up to stand. "Don't make me out to be more than I am. I'm not Norman Roxbury, and I don't intend to be," he warned. "I live by one rule, and that is, *Never* Get Close Enough To Care. I don't care about that kid or anybody else. Is that clear?"

His words were like ice water pitched in her face, and she sagged back, staring up at him in disbelief. "But— but you care about Mr. Roxbury."

"I *owe* the man, damn it. And I'm paying him back. Period."

"You're lying."

He scowled in cold fury. "Not everybody operates at gut level, Mrs. Glen. Some of us live by logic and reason."

"Don't forget greed and insensitivity!" she spat.

"Believe what you please."

She stared at him, and he stared back. The strong lines of his handsome face were rigid and uncompromising. Finally she slumped back, defeated. She'd been wrong, after all. He was not a man capable of gentleness or compassion. For whatever reason, he chose to feel nothing, to care for no one.

Listlessly she checked her watch. "It looks like you're going to be more than five minutes late, Mr. Brand. You'd better go."

Anger and fatigue skulking in his eyes, he gave a curt nod of dismissal, and pivoted away. "Maxim will see you out," he muttered.

"Don't forget. Ten sharp," she called, irritation swelling to overcome her depression. Darn it. Heart or no heart, he was going to fulfill his promise to Mr. Roxbury. At least she could see to that.

"I'll check in when I can," he said. "Tomorrow, I have a full work load."

She heard the words, but couldn't believe them. Suddenly, it was all too much. He'd gone one careless step too far. She shot to her feet. He may not have realized it, but Lucas Brand had just declared war, and the battle was on! *"Damn you!"* she sputtered, fighting tears. She was thunderstruck by the vehemence in her voice and the hollowness in her heart.

Though she was facing the window and couldn't see him, she heard his clipped footsteps pause in the vicinity of the kitchen door. Apparently he was as surprised by her stormy oath as she. From some distance away, he queried darkly, "Did you have something you wanted to add?"

Defying the censure in his tone, she spun on him. "Norman Roxbury has single-handedly headed up his Mr. Niceguy program for thirty-five years. This is the first time he's had to hand over the reins to somebody else." She found herself trudging toward him with half a mind to slap his arrogant face. "Compared to Norman Roxbury, you, Mr. Brand, are not Mr. Niceguy. You're the *flipping* Prince of Darkness!" Shakily, she sucked in a breath, so livid she felt faint. "As far as I'm concerned, there *is* no more Mr. Niceguy! If you want the whole, ugly truth, you've been nothing to me but a gigantic pain!"

Backlit by the brighter illumination in the living room, Lucas stood rooted in the doorway, tall and broad, looking as sharply elegant as a knight-errant's sword. "I'd say we're even, as far as pain goes," he ground out. "At least, for today." With the arrogant confidence she was growing accustomed to, and was highly annoyed by, he sauntered away, a man in total control.

Jess found her own emotions in just the opposite state. She was trembling helplessly, her anger so acute, so intense she could barely see for the bloodred haze that blurred her vision. *"Jackass,"* she hissed as he turned and disappeared into the entry hall.

"I've fired people for less than that," he called back.

Irked that he'd heard, she charged after him, rounding the corner to see his broad back. "Who? Your grandmother?"

He pivoted to face her, almost causing them to collide. "What did you say?" he asked, looking as though he'd heard every word, but was giving her a chance to recant before he hauled off and knocked her through one of the mirrored walls.

She swallowed, realizing she'd gone too far. You didn't go around insulting a person's gray-haired old grandmother. The fact that he'd made her furious was no excuse. "Well—" she hedged, her voice still pitched high with annoyance "—I'm sorry about that. But you make me so mad."

"That's a cross I'll have to bear," he fired back. "Now, if you'll excuse me." He turned to go.

Irate, but feeling a nagging guilt that she'd vowed to tell him something earlier and had not gotten around to it, she hurried after him, skirting around to block his path. Though her urge was to ring his neck, she compromised by merely poking violently at his tie. "Just one more thing!" She poked to emphasize every word. "Personally, I don't like you or anything you stand for, but I swore I'd say this, so I'm going to. You're a good judge of people, and I think you did the right thing in choosing Jack's essay. What smart, sarcastic comeback do you have to that?" She poked one last time, then crossed her arms defiantly.

Lucas was clearly surprised by her compliment, no matter how angrily it had been shouted. One dark brow arched in wary reaction. After a brief hesitation, he growled, "Thank you." Then, in a heartbeat, he was gone.

She stood motionless, staring at the closed door, as the sharp echo of his footsteps died away. She'd never before heard a "thank you" sound so much like "Eat dirt," before.

"Jerk-face," she snapped.

"Excuse me, madam?" came a bewildered reply from behind her. She twisted to see the austere butler, and grimaced. "I— Nothing. I was talking to myself."

She might as well have been, she mused sadly. What lunacy for her to have entertained fantasies that Lucas Brand would become Mr. Niceguy in any real sense, or that a compliment would have a positive effect. He was a flawed, reluctant figurehead, and she was stuck with him. Sighing, she gave the servant a tired smile. "Don't mind me, Maxim." She motioned for him to lead the way. "I'd better get going. I've got a lot to do."

"Yes, madam," he intoned. "Here's your case."

She was startled, having forgotten all about it. Taking it mutely, she followed him to the door. When he'd opened it for her, he ventured almost hesitantly, "Madam? Mr. Brand isn't so much of a jerk-face as you might think." His long, seamed face opened in a bashful smile. "Give him time," he suggested in a subdued rasp.

She scanned the tuxedo-clad gentleman quizzically. "Don't tell me you're fond of the man?"

The butler lifted a gray, triangular brow. "Mr. Brand may be a hard man, but he's honorable."

She shook her head in exasperation. "Well I'll agree to the 'hard' part, anyway. Good night, Maxim."

"Good night, madam," he replied as she went out into the blustery night.

THE TWO VANS THAT PULLED up into Lucas's circular drive, surrounded by well-manicured grounds, looked like something out of *The Grapes of Wrath*. They had ratty old suitcases, cardboard boxes and duffel bags tied haphazardly across their roofs as though they were a two-vehicle caravan of scraggly nomads headed out of state in search of a better life away from the dust bowl of Oklahoma. Of course that dreary image of the forty-sixth state ceased to be a fact long before these kids were born, so when Jess made the comment, she was met with blank stares.

Hopping out of the first van, Jess loped up the wide front steps to the double doors and was greeted, before she could even knock, by Jerry Jones, the skinny, grinning chauffeur, dressed in his gray uniform and soft, billed cap. He took off the hat to expose wildly curly chocolate brown hair. Jess was startled by his friendly manner. She'd never been received half so kindly by his boss, so she hadn't expected pleasantries from his employees.

"Hi, Mrs. Glen," he said. "I see you've recovered from yesterday."

When she smiled and nodded, he indicated that she follow him back down the steps. This didn't surprise her. She assumed that being the chauffeur, he'd been instructed to help with the luggage. "Mr. Brand said you should take the vehicles around the back and unload," he explained as he trotted ahead.

He hopped into the first van and led the way, then pointed to the stables and bunkhouse, which was partly masked by a stand of scrub oak. "There's where you'll be billeted. The bunkhouse hasn't been used since Mr. Brand bought the property, but the maids are gathering up some bedding. Once the kids get their gear inside, they can come on up here." He swung a gangly arm toward the house. "This door here goes into the back pantry and on to the kitchen. The bedding'll be waiting in there."

Jess was confused. "But, I thought we were to use guest rooms on the third floor."

The chauffeur's expression clouded. Evidently he'd been given instructions and no explanation. "Sorry, ma'am. I don't know about that. Want me to ask the boss?"

She shook her head, aware that Lucas was using his employee to insulate himself from his promise, while also getting the Mr. Niceguy project and its kids as far away from his exclusive domain as he could. She hadn't actually specified the main house, but Mr. Roxbury had used his own home. *Darn.* Why must she always compare Lucas Brand's behavior to Mr. Roxbury's. They were hardly comparable! With a deflated grimace, she said, "Never mind. I'll get the kids to start unloading. Thanks."

Jerry looked unhappy. "I'll ask. Maybe I misunderstood."

She shook her head. "I doubt it. I'm sure Mr. Brand thought we'd be too noisy or too messy or something, for his house. We'll be fine." She turned away, but then, having had time to get irritated, she added, "Is Mr. Brand at home?"

Jerry nodded. "Yes, ma'am. He's working in his computer room. Want me to—"

"Just tell him we're here," she interrupted, more sharply than she'd intended. Calming herself, she smiled with difficulty. "I'll want to talk to him in about an hour."

Jerry nodded and started for the back door, when she stopped him, calling out, "And please—call me Jess."

He looked over his shoulder. "I'm Jerry to my friends." He grinned at her. Jerry had a weakly handsome face. His chin was pointy, and his eyes too small for a man his height—just over six feet. But they were clear, blue eyes, alight with friendship and sympathy. "You're doing a fine thing, ma'am—I mean, Jess. Good luck. And let me know if I can help. I got a police scanner, if you need it."

She appreciated his offer. "Thanks, Jerry. I'll keep it in mind. What do you use a police scanner for?"

He turned back to face her and shrugged his broad, thin shoulders. "Oh, I hear stuff about shootings, robberies, runaways." He thudded his thumb into his uniform front. "I figure if I'm lucky, I'll get on 'Unsolved Mysteries' for catching a serial killer or something." He must have seen a trace of doubt in her expression, for he added, "Honest. We got plenty of crime here in OK City."

She had to agree with that. "Well—thanks for the offer. And if you hear of any serial killers in the area, let us know."

He laughed. "You're kiddin', but I will. Also, I'm great with spaghetti sauce, if your kids need a good recipe. My day off's Sunday."

She grew vaguely hopeful. "Oh? You mean Mr. Brand doesn't go to work on Sundays?"

Jerry shook his head, clapping his hat back on. "Naw. He goes. He's got the ragin' red Testarossa."

She made a face. "Sounds painful."

Jerry looked baffled, then laughed his high-pitched, staccato laugh. "The red Testarossa's Mr. Brand's Ferrari." He took on the look of a lovesick pup. "Heck. If I had one of them, I'd fire me and drive that baby all the time."

Light laughter bubbled in Jess's throat. "I'd be glad he isn't you, then. You'd be out of a job." Secretly, she would have preferred that Lucas Brand *was* Jerry—at least his attitude toward the Mr. Niceguy project would be a trillion-percent better.

"Well—be seein' ya. I'll give that message to the boss," Jerry promised as he jogged toward the door leading to the kitchen.

"Thanks," she replied, then headed back to the van to direct the kids to the bunkhouse where they'd been banished. The volunteer couples, Howie and Reba Goodall, both retired teachers, and Bertha and Bernie Kornblum, who owned a small farm outside of town, cast each other subtle glances of disappointment. They recognized the ostracism for what it was, just as Jess had. But as the kids scrambled around untying their stuff, laughing and shouting, nudging, teasing and generally horsing around, Jess silently prayed that they wouldn't recognize the rejection. The six boys and four girls had already known enough of that in their young lives.

The bunkhouse was a long, one-story building with a wood-shingled roof and walls constructed of rough-cut pine treated with a reddish stain. Wooden shutters were closed across the windows, making it obvious that the place had been locked up for some time. Jess hoped it wouldn't require much cleaning. The kids shouldn't have to slave over their accommodations. This wasn't a construction site or a prison camp. It was a retreat and supposedly a time to fish, to ride horses, to collect leaves or jump in them; a time to run, to learn how to work together as a team, be a family, be creative, see how life could be better, and basically, to enjoy a reward for having tried and succeeded at something.

Jess took a suitcase in each hand and struggled to join Annie Smith and Suzy Clark, who were loaded down with bags. Moses Booker raced past Jess and the two girls, each with a duffel bag under one arm and a suitcase grasped in the other hand. "I'm gonna check this place out. You comin', Spitball?"

Jess had to smile. The Asian boy, Noriko Sakata, had been given the nickname Spitball, and she had no idea why. She supposed it was best that she didn't. Noriko was a native of Oklahoma City. His dad, an immigrant, had died several years before, and his mother, not proficient in English, was having a hard time making ends meet for herself and her three sons. Spitball was a good kid, worked two part-time jobs after school, and had done well on the essay. He was slight, with spiky black hair and a bighearted grin.

"I'm coming, dude," Spitball puffed, dragging the biggest suitcase of the bunch. Jess shook her head at him. For a kid of fourteen who was just under five feet tall and couldn't possibly weigh one hundred pounds yet, Spitball had no idea he wasn't as strong and big as an ox.

Jack lagged behind, not speaking, but doing his share. He had single-handedly lifted a cooker off the top of van number two. It had to weigh eighty pounds, but Jack was carrying it stoically and uncomplainingly. The teen was big for fourteen. Jess was five-seven, and Jack was about an inch taller, but he outweighed her by fifty pounds of muscle.

She dropped back so he could catch up. "Now that's what I call helping," she said to him. "I have this recipe for hamburger patties that'll curl your hair. It has jalapeño peppers in it. Sound good?"

He peered suspiciously at her. "Sounds gross."

She stopped to adjust her grip on one suitcase. "I knew you'd love the idea."

"Hey," shouted Annie, the black girl who looked remarkably like Janet Jackson, but whose shiny black hair was done Medusa-style. "Door's stuck or something!" she called.

"They didn't give me a key, so it shouldn't be locked." Jess hurried through the thick stand of trees that partly hid the bunkhouse. "Just a second."

When she got there, Moses, the other black essay winner, was tugging hard. "Don't mess wif me, man," he was grumbling at the door. One more hard tug, and there was a skin-crawling rasping sound as the swollen wood scraped against the concrete porch and the door swung open.

Since the windows were shuttered, it was dark inside. Moses was the first to venture in, searching the nearby wall for a light switch. When he found it, several naked bulbs that hung from the peaked ceiling flashed on to reveal a sitting room/kitchen combination. Farther back, behind half-wall planters, long empty of anything green and living, there were several sets of bunk beds, each with a bare mattress.

As Moses looked around, he was joined by Larry Tenkiller, Annie and Suzy. Jess stepped forward to get a better look.

"Cool," said Larry.

"Are we all sleeping together?" Suzy, a chubby, pink-cheeked blonde breathed nervously.

"Radical!" Larry piped up, with a bawdy laugh. "Let's scope this place out."

"I'm not sleeping in the same room with these buttheads!" Suzy griped.

"Chill, girl," Moses rebuked, nudging Spitball. "You ain't all that fine that I'd mess with you."

Jess stared at the accommodations—certainly not suitable for *both* boys and girls. "We'll figure out something," she mumbled, her irritation flaring again. How could Lucas Brand have been so insensitive? "I can tell you right now," she added, "there will be no coed sleeping on this retreat."

Howie had come in. "Let's get the windows open, boys," he suggested. "And you girls look for the broom closet."

"Good idea," Jess said, glad to have something for the kids to do while the adults put their heads together to figure out how to arrange the place to separate the boys from the girls. She had an unruly urge to smack Lucas's arrogant face for his thoughtlessness.

The kids scurried about, their footsteps thudding heavily on the plank floor. Windows were unlatched and sunshine poured in to display the thick layer of dust that had settled over everything. It was just as Jess had feared. The kids would have no fun today. *Darn you, Lucas Brand!*

She and the other volunteers tried to hide their disgust with smiles and hearty facades as the kids began the cleanup campaign to ready the grubby, musty bunkhouse for the week's activities ahead.

Jess was sweeping between a couple of sets of bunk beds when she stopped suddenly and looked around, wrinkling her nose. Something smelled. . . .

"*Aaargh! Lorda-mercy!*" squealed Annie, who stood stock still with her broom in midair a few yards away from Jess. "A polecat's shot his stink off in here!"

The smell was strong, almost debilitating. Jess's eyes began to burn and it was hard to breathe.

There were other cries and curses flying around, as youngsters and volunteers alike dropped whatever they were doing and raced for the door. Jess was shoved against a bunk, and fell sideways on it, coughing and wiping her eyes.

The crawl space had apparently become the home of one or more skunks—angry, vengeance-seeking skunks.

Jess got to her feet and stumbled to the door, scrambling out with the rest of the victims.

Her eyes were watering like leaky hoses as she looked around. Some of the kids had taken off for the main house, running as if their clothes were on fire.

Well, it wasn't as life-threatening as fire, but the experience was as horrible in its own way. The rest of the kids were standing around, some wailing, some choking from the stench they were giving off. Annie had to be forcibly restrained from peeling out of her putrid-smelling clothes right there on the lawn.

Jess wiped at her eyes, glaring at the main residence with complete and utter contempt.

"Come on, kids," she announced loudly, beckoning toward Lucas Brand's precious, nice-smelling house. "We have to get out of these clothes and get de-skunked." Heading across the lawn, she muttered, "It's time to inform Mr. Niceguy he's about to have some *very ripe* company."

6

JESS TRAMPED THROUGH the kitchen, where several teenagers huddled, sniveling and grumbling. Members of the Brand staff peered out from around corners, their noses pinched tightly to stave off the foul odor.

Maxim hurried to catch up as Jess trekked across the carpeted grand room. The butler hid his nose behind a white handkerchief. "Perhaps I should announce you, Mrs. Glen," he suggested through the linen as he rushed to catch up with her enraged pace.

"I don't imagine I'll need to be announced, Maxim," she called back. "He'll detect me soon enough. Where is he?" She paused long enough in the middle of the great room to glance back over her shoulder. Maxim cast a worried look toward the entrance hall.

"That way?" she asked, heading for it.

"Yes ma'am," he rasped, pursuing her like a protective mother hen determined to defend her chick. "I really should tell him—"

"Oh, please," she cut in. "Let me surprise him." She ran a hand, quivering with fury, through her reeking hair. "You said he wasn't so bad, Maxim. Let's find out, shall we?"

The butler's forehead creased with uncertainty but after a few seconds, he indicated the direction with a reluctant nod. "At the head of the hall," he told her gloomily, "instead of turning right into the foyer toward the main entrance, you turn left. There's a circular staircase to the second floor. Over the garage there's a big room—"

"I'll find it." She dashed down the hallway toward the mirrored entranceway, then hung a quick left through another set of double doors. Inside was a small carpeted area with a corkscrew staircase that wound tightly up to another level. She took the steps two at a time, in part out of pent-up fury, in part to escape her own stench.

The second landing was simply that. A landing. One window with beige miniblinds looked out over the side yard. A pair of beige upholstered chairs on either side of the window were there no doubt for people stuck cooling their heels, waiting to see Mr. Wonderful, cloistered in his hallowed computer room.

Jess didn't intend to wait one single second for Lucas Brand. She burst through the door into a long, simply furnished, open room. The walls were white, with white window shades raised to allow the sun in. The pinewood floor gleamed in the spots where it could be seen between the piles and streamers of crumpled computer printouts that were strewn about. This startled her, for it was so uncharacteristic of Lucas.

A man sat at the far end of the room. Jess couldn't be one-hundred-percent sure it was Lucas because his head was almost completely hidden by an oversize helmet of some sort with a protuberance at the front. A Donald Duck space helmet came to mind. Wires connected to the back of the headgear led to computer equipment that was beeping, flashing and purring in a semicircle about him.

For the first time, Jess had an inkling of the hightech world Lucas spent his time in. She was impressed by the intelligence it must require to be on the cutting edge of such advanced technology but disturbed by the foreign nature of what she saw. It seemed like a world more suited to alien beings than the warm, fuzzy sort of world she craved.

She peered curiously at him. He was groping around in empty air, his right hand encased in a silver glove that might have once belonged to Michael Jackson. Lucas was maneuvering the glove in the vacant space above his desktop. "Okay, baby, stay with me. Take me all the way—that's good. No, no, hell—don't stop. You damn tease."

He grew silent, squeezed the gloved hand again, then sat back, saying, "Okay, that's better. Now, let's see if we can keep it hard if I torque around while I squeeze."

Jess's cheeks went hot. What had she blundered into? It sounded so—so lewd. What was he doing? She'd never heard of any sex toys that required a Donald Duck hood and a Michael Jackson glove. But Lucas seemed to be getting some sort of gratification out of the experience. She swallowed, not sure she wanted to know if Mr. Lucas Brand had a high-tech, perverted side to his personality. Then she thought of Miss Mary Anne Brown, who'd seemed so lovesick in the restaurant. Apparently he wasn't kinky enough to turn women off—

"No—*no*," he groused, drawing the glove back. He'd resumed talking to himself, under his breath. Or to some mechanical, invisible girlfriend . . .

"Let me, babe. Don't fight me—don't—*Damn. . . .*" His words died abruptly, and he tilted in his swivel chair. "What the hell . . ." he muttered, cocking his hel-muted head. When he'd turned far enough around so Jess could see his mouth, she noticed with some satis-faction that he was frowning. Clearly the skunk odor had finally reached him.

She remained quiet, banking her anger with diffi-culty as he used his free hand to lift off the helmet. When he saw Jess standing there, his scowl deepened. "What *is* that?"

"It's only me," she said, giving him her most inno-cent, wide-eyed stare. "Sorry to disturb you and your-er-hand. I hope I didn't spoil the mood, but I wanted you to know we're here."

"I can *smell* you're here," he said, stripping off the glove. "What happened? You stink like you fell in a cesspool."

She walked toward him nonchalantly. "Really? Maybe it's my new perfume. It's called Obscene."

"The name fits. It smells obscene."

"You think so?" She gave him a puzzled stare. "A few brands turn funny on some skins. Maybe this scent isn't right for me."

"It's more suited to chemical warfare." He stood. "I'd get my money back, if I were you." Brows dipping in disgust, he held up a hand to halt her. "Don't come any closer."

She ignored his command, drawing near to trace a finger along the helmet. She noticed that he backed a few steps away, and she felt a spiteful satisfaction. "What were you doing?" she asked. "Sounded very risqué. Is it some sort of space-age sex for singles?"

"I'd need more than a glove for that." He coughed and she was sure it was due to her foul-smelling nearness. "What happened to you?" he asked, looking pained.

She couldn't stand the game any longer. She'd wanted him to suffer at least a little, but there were fourteen miserable people downstairs who needed immediate help. "I'll tell you what happened," she hissed. "Mr. Niceguy—maybe you've heard of him? Well, he banished us to a closed-up bunkhouse that had been infested by a pack of skunks. That's what happened. And now there are a whole lot of smelly, pitiful people crowded in your kitchen in need of de-skunking." She planted her fists on her hips. "I'll bet there's a proverb for people who treat people like you treated us today. Something like, 'Stinkers shall *reap* what they sow.' But in your case it's *reek!*"

She headed toward the door. "Start figuring out where we'll be staying, Mr. Niceguy, 'cause Bernie, our volunteer who grew up on a farm and knows skunks, says that bunkhouse won't be livable for weeks."

"HOW MUCH TOMATO JUICE?" Jerry asked as he headed out the door, clearly grateful to be given a job that required his absence.

"All they have. Get cases," Lucas growled. "And get it back here fast."

"Yes, sir," Jerry shouted on the run.

Jess was perched on the edge of the kitchen table, making a list of needed items. She glanced at Lucas, who was barking orders to a staff who were scurrying around like frenzied ants, their noses clutched between thumb and index finger, or covered by perfumed kerchiefs.

Lucas had removed his suit coat and had loosened his tie, apparently his mode of attire for emergencies. He was angry, but she had to give him credit—he was very much in command.

The boys had been divided between two bathrooms. Howie was directing the cleaning of one group and Bernie the other. The girls had been ushered into two bathrooms in the far wing, with Bertha and Reba in charge. Servants were dutifully clearing the pantry of all tomato products on hand, since Bernie had said tomato juice was the best skunk-odor remover he'd found, in years of trying both commercial products and home remedies.

Jess hadn't yet had a chance to deodorize herself. She'd been hurriedly composing a list for Lucas. "Okay," she said, pulling his attention away from his staff's progress. "The girls' suitcases were all that had been brought inside the bunkhouse, so you'll only have to pick up things for them. Unless you'd rather help get rooms ready and send one of the maids."

Lucas tossed her a quarrelsome glare, making it very clear he wasn't a man who did hospital corners on beds unless held at gunpoint. "I've never bought clothes for fourteen-year-old girls. What in blazes do you expect me to do?"

She shoved the list at him. "Ask a saleslady. Tell her there're four, and they're all fourteen. One's plump, the others are average. And don't forget underwear."

Lucas winced, "You're loving this, aren't you?"

She lifted her chin, her expression defiant. "Which part? Where I smell like a sewage-processing plant or get to marinate in a tub of cold vegetable juice?" She sniffed contemptuously. "You're so clever to see through me. I've always had a secret urge to masquerade as a Swiss steak."

His jaw clenched, but he didn't say anything else, just walked away and disappeared around a corner.

Jess eyed the spot where he'd been standing, and her lips twitched. "Actually—yes, Mr. Brand," she whispered. "For your information, I *am* loving turning you into an errand boy!"

She then went upstairs to check on Bertha's progress with the tomato-paste shampoo she was giving Suzy Clark. The whining Jess had heard wasn't a good sign. Poor kids. Served Lucas right to go through the embarrassment of buying girl's underwear. She found herself grinning, wishing she could be there to bask in his humiliation. Her attitude was harsh, she supposed. But she was only human—a human that smelled like rotten eggs. Small acts of revenge were probably forgivable under the circumstances.

It was another hour before Jess had a chance to bathe, for she insisted everyone else clean up first. Thirty minutes earlier, Jerry had returned with boxes and boxes of tomato juice, crushed tomatoes and tomato sauce, having cleaned out the local Super Grocery Circus's complete stockpile of tomato products. It had turned out to be barely enough.

Now, Jess was dressed, but her hair was wrapped in a towel as she waited her turn at a blow dryer. She met Lucas in the kitchen where he dumped stacks of brown department-store sacks on the table.

"Good, you're finally back. The girls are upstairs wrapped in blankets watching sitcom reruns," she informed him. "How'd you do?"

He pursed his lips with annoyance, then ground out, "It was about as humiliating as you wanted it to be."

She hid her amusement by bending to open a bag. In the midst of rummaging through jeans, socks and sweatshirts, she stopped, stunned. "What in heaven's name...?"

Gingerly, she pulled out a scrap of black lace that turned out to be a skimpy, indecent excuse for a bra. Examining it more closely, she realized the garment was big enough for the most well-endowed exotic dancer in Las Vegas, let alone Oklahoma. She stared, tongue-tied, for a long moment.

"What's wrong?" he asked. "It's underwear."

"For who, Bumpers Bambi from the Exotic Strip-tease Inn on Highway 7?" She turned to stare at him. "This is your idea of what a fourteen-year-old girl wears under her Bart Simpson sweatshirt?"

"I told the saleslady to give me a bra in every size. Maybe this color was the only one in—"

"I see," Jess interrupted, stuffing it back into the bag. "Well, we won't be needing the industrial-strength model. These girls haven't had the cosmetic surgery required to fit this one." She scanned the rest of the contents of the black-and-gold sack, her eyes widening. "For heaven's sake, Lucas. They're all see-through black lace. Where did you buy these things, anyway?"

"The lingerie shop in the mall."

"Damian's Delightful Undies." She shook her head, incredulous, then found herself struggling not to laugh. "Didn't the red garter belts in the window give you any clues...?" She couldn't go on. The situation was too crazy. He'd tried, she supposed, and had done as well as any bachelor—whose idea of women's underwear probably didn't even include the word *serviceable*.

Glancing back at him, she managed with an almost-straight face, "For future reference, try a JC Penney or Sears store, and get plain cotton in white or pink."

He frowned, detecting her amusement. "On what frozen day in Hades do you anticipate I'll need that information?"

She shook her head, grabbing up the sack. "Never mind." She started out of the kitchen, then stopped. He'd made such an adorable human error—so utterly, ineptly male and out of character. Turning around, she said, "I was wrong to criticize, Lucas. You tried. I'll tell the girls Damian's was having a sale. They'll understand the concept of buying something tasteless because it's cheap and it was an emergency."

"Tasteless?" he repeated, sounding hurt.

She nodded. "I'm afraid so.

He frowned, muttering, "And they weren't cheap. I don't see why you have to lie."

She let out a small chuckle, unable to help herself. All of a sudden, Lucas Brand wasn't the great and powerful wizard of ROMs or RAMs or megawhatevers. He was simply a man helplessly out of his element in a world of women's lace and frills. Kind of cute . . .

Worriedly, she shook off her unexpected softening. "It's either lie about a sale, or have four fourteen-year-old girls believing you bought them sexy underwear because you think they're sexy, date material. Is that what you want from pubescent females who're already calling you a hot babe?"

"Hell, that's the last thing I need," he groused. "Tell them they were free, if you want."

She shrugged. "A fifty-percent-off sale will do."

He leaned a hip against the table. "What in hell would make them think of me as a hot babe? I've hardly even spoken to them."

Her smile faded. "Don't be coy, Lucas," she retorted, feeling irked. "You know you're handsome. You're rich. And acting brooding and silent makes you seem mysterious. The combination of good looks, money and mystery is hard to resist—at any age." She bit her tongue. What had made her add that last part? She'd have given anything to take the words back, and was horrified to see the amusement that flickered in his dark eyes.

"Why, thank you, Jess." His grin was as taunting as his tone.

Darn him. Somehow, he'd gotten the misguided notion that she was intrigued by him! *Egomaniac!* She stiffened, and spun away, grumbling "Give me strength."

DARKNESS HAD FALLEN and it was chilly. The teens, bundled in parkas, were divided into two teams of five kids. Each team member was armed with a gunnysack.

"Okay, folks," Jess said, "Howie and Reba will chase the snipes with team one, and Mr. Niceguy and I will do it with team two. Whichever team catches the most snipes in their gunnysacks by midnight, gets a prize.

Howie and Reba, carrying sticks about two feet long, recently cut from a nearby scrub oak, set off to lead their crew to a remote section of Lucas's wooded property. Lucas and Jess were similarly equipped, ready to lead their group in another direction.

"When we get back at midnight, Bertha and Bernie will have a snack ready for us, and we'll award the prize to the winning team." Jess grinned. "And don't try to find out what the prize is, or you forfeit it to the other team."

The kids on these retreats were always excited—too excited to sleep on their first night. So, they got to go on a "snipe hunt." Little did they know it was all a joke—that there were no such fuzzy little animals as snipes. Several kinds of long-billed sandpipers called snipes inhabited marshy areas of Eurasia and North America, but none of those birds resided anywhere near Oklahoma City. The boys and girls, however, didn't know that. And the game had always served as a fun icebreaker, giving everybody a laugh.

Lucas, however, wasn't laughing. When the teenagers were out of earshot, he rumbled under his breath, "So, you and I are supposed to leave these kids in the woods for two hours, alone?

She nodded, swishing her stick at the fallen leaves. "You can run back to the house and play with your hand again, if you want to. I'll hang around and keep an eye on them."

"Don't you think this little prank is cruel? I mean, it's cold out here."

She shushed him with a finger to her lips. "They'll get a good laugh out of it, and any embarrassment will be salved by Bertha's pecan pie. Both have been a staple of these retreats for five years, and they've always been a hit."

Lucas shrugged. "I won't argue with an armed woman."

He wasn't all that easy to see beneath the canopy of branches, though many of the trees had lost most of their leaves. Still, the autumn three-quarter moon was bright enough for Jess to detect his expression of displeasure.

"Okay, team," she enthused. "Remember the snipe mating-call sounds like the chattering noise we practiced. You know, putting your tongue against the back of your front teeth and sucking as you pull your tongue away—like this." She demonstrated, making a noise that sounded like, *thit-thit-thit.*

Annie Smith tried it. Then Suzy Clark joined in. Moses Booker laughed at the girls. "Oh, man, scope out the tongue action on these babes."

"Yeah?" quipped Annie, with a reproving look. "Well, you'd better scope it out, 'cause that's as close as you're gonna get to *my* tongue."

Jess laughed. "Okay, let's hear your snipe call, Moses."

"Yeah. Let's hear it," Annie said with a smirk. "Mr. Tongue Action."

"Come on, you guys. Maybe the prize is money. Let's catch some snipes," Suzy chimed in. Turning to Jack, she said, "Let's you and me partner up."

Jess exchanged a knowing glance with Lucas. It was painfully clear that Suzy had designs on the silent, sulking Jack.

Lucas whispered, "This was a great idea. Fourteen-year-old couples groping in the woods."

Jess ignored him and reminded the kids, "No breaking off into little groups. There are wild things out here."

"Like, besides Moses?" Annie chimed in sarcastically.

"Hey, don't disrespect me, woman," Moses complained. "You might be glad I'm around if a bear shows up."

"I doubt if that will happen," Jess said. "You five stay in a group. Mr. Niceguy and I are going out to beat the bushes. You make the snipe call, and be ready to nab them in your sacks. Remember, be gentle with them. We're only going to catch them, feed them some honey and bread, then let them go. We've never had more than ten caught, so there's an extra prize if you beat the record."

"Radical," Larry Tenkiller said. "My ancestors hunted the plains hundreds of years ago. You guys otta be glad I'm here. Native Americans are great trackers."

"Oh yeah?" Moses cut in. "What tribe are you, my man—Last of the Mo' Stupids?"

"You're real funny, dork," Larry said. "Just watch me, and learn."

"Heap big dwebe," Jack groused, too quietly for Larry to hear, but Jess caught it.

She ignored the grumble, and nodded to Lucas. "Get to making the snipe mating-call. We're off to whack the bushes."

When they'd angled off through some trees, Lucas said, "Whacking bushes sounds dirty."

"Depends on where you keep your mind." Jess lifted her stick to rest it on her shoulder. "Why don't you go on back to the house and whack anything you want," she suggested. She glanced down at her watch. "You have one hour and forty-five minutes."

"And what are you going to do?"

"Hang around and watch to make sure that Suzy doesn't attack Jack, or Moses doesn't get any tongue action other than snipe calling."

"You'll get lost."

She peered up at him. The moonlight made his dark eyes sparkle. She wondered how that was possible, but decided it wasn't something she ought to dwell on out here in the dark, alone with him. "I—I dropped bread crumbs," she lied unsteadily.

"What about the wild things that you warned the kids about? Aren't you afraid of them?"

"What do I really have to fear out here, except skunks?"

"You could fall and break your leg. Sometimes we have wild dogs in the woods. Hungry, wild dogs."

Casually he put a hand into his jeans pocket—or his chauffeur's jeans pocket. Whomever they belonged to, they fit him all too well, and Jess couldn't help giving him a glance. "Well, " she admitted haltingly, "I'm not a woodswoman, if that's what you're getting at. But, I doubt if I'll have any real problems. Besides, I know you're a busy man. You keep reminding me. So go."

He pursed his lips, seeming to consider her offer. "This is unlike you," he said. "Ever since we met, you've been on my case about not being around to help. Now, suddenly, you can't get rid of me fast enough."

He was perceptive. The last person she wanted to be alone with in the woods was Lucas Brand. She'd maneuvered every which way not to be partnered with him, but as usual, she'd failed.

The Goodalls had been sweet, but they'd insisted that they were always partners, and Bertha had claimed she couldn't possible make the piecrust without Bernie's help. It was his grandmother's recipe, and only he could make the darned stuff flaky enough. So Jess had been forced to make this trek into the woods with a man whose company she objected to with all her heart.

"Don't you have a meeting or a phone call or Trekkie sex games or something?" she asked, sounding pitifully hopeful.

"Very funny." He shook his head. "Actually, Sol and Fletch have been in the office for forty-eight hours straight. I told them to get some sleep and a bath. We have a conference call at six in the morning."

"Well, then," she suggested, "you go on back and get some sleep or a bath."

He grinned down at her. "Why, has my after-shave soured on me?"

He'd come very close to the truth. Only his after-shave hadn't *soured*, but it had certainly been bothersome. Every time he drew near, she got a heady whiff of him, and he smelled awfully good—hot, spicy and all male. Grimly, she fibbed, "I hadn't noticed."

"Then what's your problem? Are you afraid I'll attack you, or something?"

"Certainly not!" she blurted, disgusted that she sounded so frightened. "This is a stupid conversation. I need to sneak up and check on the kids. I'm afraid the black lace undies you bought for the girls have gone to Suzy's head, and she's dying to show hers off." Jess wheeled around, forgetting that her stick was resting on her shoulder. She felt the stick knock hard against something, and twisted back, horrified. She saw Lucas put a protective hand over his eye. "Oh, my goodness," she cried in a whisper. "I hit you!"

He was shaking his head, as though to try to clear his vision. "I noticed," he grunted under his breath.

"How bad is it? Should we rush you to a hospital?" She was terrified that she might have destroyed his vision. "I'm so sorry." She brushed away his hand and gently holding the lids apart, peered up into the injured eye. "I can't see much," she said. "It's too dark. We'd better get to some light."

She took his hand and began to drag him along. "I hope I didn't scratch the cornea, but I hear they can do wonderful things with laser surgery these days. I'm sure—" Her voice broke, and she sucked in a shuddery breath.

An instant later, she was facing him. Somehow he'd turned her around and was looking down at her sternly, one eye nearly closed. "Look, Jess," he began seriously, "I'm fine. I don't think it hit my eye, just grazed the lid. I'll probably be bruised tomorrow, but I'm not really hurt. So shut up."

He held her by her upper arms and shook her slightly. She swallowed, a little less panicky. "Are you sure? I mean, I'd never forgive myself if I'd maimed you."

He gave a short laugh. "You're a strange case, Mrs. Glen. You don't mind screwing me out of a hundred million dollars, but you go all to pieces when you think you've scratched me. Why is that? Don't you know I'd endure one hell of a lot of physical pain for that kind of money?"

She stared up into his beguiling features. He didn't seem angry or even irritated; just mildly curious about the workings of her mind. And there was something else there, too. It wasn't so much in the way he looked at her or his words, but the fact that he was holding her arms—gently, and for no good reason anymore. Her gaze slid to the ground. "Do you mean for one hundred million dollars you'd allow yourself to be blinded?"

"No, of course not," he jeered. "But you're not even slightly remorseful about the business crisis your Mr. Niceguy thing is causing me, and yet a little poke in my eye has you in tears."

"Don't be crazy!" she objected, embarrassed, unhappily aware that she'd been near tears a minute ago. He must have seen the telltale glimmer in her eyes, reflected by the dratted moonlight.

He frowned at her for another minute, then half smiled. It was a cynical look. "Good," he said flatly. "Let's keep it that way. I don't want anyone crying on my account."

Jess sensed that there was a postscript to his remark, unspoken yet very clear. *And I don't intend to become close enough to anyone else to cry for them, either.*

Jess knew it would be foolhardy to make any comment, but for some reason, she longed to ask him what had made him so cold and remote.

Before she had a chance to open her mouth and insert her foot, somebody screamed.

7

AFTER THE SECOND SCREAM, Jess realized that it was more like a squeal and was coming from a young girl.

"I think Annie changed her attitude about Moses's tongue action," Lucas said, heading in the direction of the noise.

"Oh, Lord," Jess muttered uneasily. She only hoped the foreplay hadn't gone too far. They'd never had this sort of difficulty on a retreat before.

"Okay," Lucas was saying to someone Jess still couldn't see when she caught up. "What's all the shouting about?"

Moses and Annie were half hidden in a scattering of leaves, but at the the sound of Lucas's voice, Annie bolted up, hurriedly zipping her new lilac parka. "I—I tripped," she stuttered, supporting herself with a hand on her companion's shoulder. "Moses was helping—me—er—up...."

"I'd say he was helping *something* up," Lucas said, tossing his stick aside. "Let me give you a hand, Mr. Booker." Without waiting for the boy to reply, he took hold of his upper arm and hauled him to his feet.

"Hey!" Moses objected. "Don't trip, man. I wasn't raping the woman. We were just having some fun."

"Yeah?" Lucas released the boy. "From *that* kind of fun comes babies. You want a baby?"

Moses shifted uneasily, and his face caught a shaft of bright moonlight. Jess could see his expression change from aggravated to troubled. "I don't want no babies, man!"

Jess had taken Annie's hand. The girl was mortified, whimpering, "Gee, Mrs. Glen, we wouldn't have— wouldn't have done—you know—*the wild thing*. I swear."

Jess felt a rush of depression about the foolishness of teenagers, but tried to smile. "That's how a lot of babies get started, Annie. Terribly, terribly unplanned." She looked around. "Where's your gunnysack?"

Annie sniffed and wiped her nose with the back of her hand. "I think it's over there."

"Lead the way." Jess had a feeling Lucas wanted to talk to Moses alone. She was the one trained for such a task, but she sensed that Moses might respond better to a man, since he had no male role model in his family.

She cast Lucas a worried look over her shoulder, wondering what he would say. Deciding she'd better keep her ears open, she whispered to Annie, "You find that sack and join Jack, Suzy and Larry." She could see the three of them huddled not far away. "You kids get on with the hunt. This delay may cost you the championship if you hang around doing nothing. I'll get my stick and start beating the bushes." She decided it was time to tell a real whopper. "I saw a couple of snipes running that way." She pointed directly away from Moses and Lucas. "Get over there about ten yards or so, and keep your eyes peeled."

Annie grabbed her sack and joined the other team members. As they disappeared into the shadow-shrouded woods, Jess stealthily made her way back to hide behind a beech tree. She prayed Lucas would be as good at man-to-man talks as he was at making money, but had her doubts.

"Okay, Moses," Lucas was saying. "I know where you're coming from. You're feeling your hormones. It's normal."

The youth grunted, but made no comment.

"You've got to use your brains along with your..." There was a pause, and Jess chewed the inside of her cheek in nervous anticipation. After a second, Lucas continued, "Along with Mr. Prick, down there."

"A lot you know, man. You're *old*," Moses groused. "And Annie's a fine thing—hot to trot."

"I don't care if she's a racehorse that's been set on fire, you *don't* have sex with her. Not this week, and not unprotected. There are diseases out there, man, that can cut your horny little life short. You get me?"

Silence reigned for so long, Jess had to venture a look. Moses' expression was masked by darkness. Lucas's face was visible, however, and he appeared serious, but not angry. His hand was on the boy's shoulder. Jess was startled by the humanness of the action, and wondered if it was pretense, or if he really wanted to help Moses.

"But she— But Annie came on to me, man..." Moses carped, breaking into Jess's musings.

"With a stud like you, it'll happen again." Lucas half grinned in understanding. "And when that day comes, have a condom in your wallet. Protect yourself and the girl."

Moses frowned. "I ain't got the bread for condoms."

"Do you have the bread to feed a baby, or are you one of those jerks who screws 'em and leaves 'em?"

Moses met Lucas's eyes. "My old man did that. Left my mom before I was born."

"And he's your idol?"

"He's a *badass*."

"You want to be like your dad?"

"Get off my back, man."

"Answer my question," Lucas prodded. "Do you want to be an ass to some other little boy someday?"

Moses made a pained face. "No. I want to be a car designer."

"Good goal." Lucas patted his shoulder. "Tell you what. Before you leave, I'll give you some condoms. You use them when Mr. Prick goes into action, and you stay in school. One day, you just may be an automotive designer."

Moses peered sideways at Lucas, his expression skeptical. "You're gonna give me rubbers?"

"Don't tell Mrs. Glen. I'm not sure it's part of the program."

Lucas smiled then—a warm, amused, open smile. Jess stared, dismayed at how her heart thrilled at the sight.

Moses chuckled suddenly, and shook his head as though incredulous. "You're a cool dude, Mr. Nice-guy." He stuck out a hand. "And I thought you were a total dwebe."

Lucas took the boy's hand. "Even dwebes have their Mr. Prick days."

Moses bent to pick up Lucas's snipe stick. "Here. I guess I'll go scope out the bushes for them furry little farts. Thanks for not beating my butt, man."

"Pleasure's all mine."

Moses ambled off, whooshing his stick through the fallen leaves as he went. Jess flattened herself against the tree, holding her breath. She didn't want Moses or Lucas to know she'd been eavesdropping.

"How'd I do?" came a soft question from very nearby.

Jess jumped and spun to find Lucas lounging against the tree beside her, his expression amused.

She swallowed, ashamed that he'd caught her. "How did you know I was here?"

He shrugged his sinfully wide shoulders.

"I figured, with you being a mother-hen sort of woman, you'd be hovering nearby," he explained. "Also, since you don't like me, I knew you'd be ready to pounce the minute I made a wrong move."

Her face grew warm with embarrassment. "Am I that transparent?

"You're cellophane." He paused, then added, "So, since you didn't leap out of the bushes at me, I gather I did okay."

She shoved her hands into her pockets. "I could have done without the 'Mr. Prick' comment, but other than that, you did okay."

"I'm gratified. And the free condom offer?"

He was teasing her now. She decided two could play at this game. Defiantly she asked, "What do you want, a *hand?*" Drawing tense fists from her coat pockets, she unclenched them, and pressed her palms together slowly and deliberately, three times. "Happy now?"

"Why didn't you want to come with me, tonight?"

Startled by his abrupt change of subject, she sputtered, "Why—I—never . . ."

"I heard you begging Reba to let you go with Howie. And I have a feeling it's not because you have a raging crush on the man. My gut tells me it was because you're afraid of me."

"Well—your gut's crazy!" she retorted in a voice too high-pitched to be believed.

"Why are you so afraid of me?" he coaxed, leaning closer.

She took a step away from him. "I—I'm not afraid, Mr. Brand," she hedged, with rising panic. Angry that he could make her so defensive, she fell back, as she invariably did, on the unvarnished truth. No matter how hurtful it might be, she plunged on blindly. "If you *must* know, I'm not at ease around type *A*s, like you. My father was one, my mother was one, my husband was one. I'm tired of being the loser in every situation. I don't like to be manipulated, belittled, having to always be on guard. You aggressive I-have-to-be-the-winner-no-matter-who-I-step-on people make me feel—feel—mediocre—"

Her voice broke with the shame of having to admit her failing to a man who didn't know the meaning of the word. She swallowed, hurrying on, "And—and anxious. That's why I work with needy kids. That's why I'm in a field that calls for gentleness, allows victories to be small—*human* ones. That's why—"

She found herself swept into a bold embrace and felt Lucas's strength surround her as his lips came down to taste her mouth. Neither the kiss, nor his touch were harsh or demanding as she might have expected them to be. He was tender and compelling, and she was suddenly, mindlessly, leaning against him, relishing the pressure of his hands, the sexy maleness of his hard frame, the unexpected sweetness of his lips.

Somehow she had the impression he wasn't so much interested in conquering her as comforting her—an odd feeling to have, considering the type of man he was. She hadn't imagined he had a comforting bone in his body, but her flustered tirade seemed to have struck some obscure, gentle chord deep inside the man. She sensed that even Lucas was startled by his desire to console, for his lips caressed hers, featherlike, charmingly hesitant.

Well aware that she would be foolish to allow this to go on, she tried to put an end to their unanticipated intimacy, but her senses betrayed her. The power and scent of him was disarming. As his mouth shifted seductively over hers, a small sound of wonder escaped her throat. His lips, though potent and clever, were surprisingly sensitive as they moved, and she responded by relaxing, reciprocating in kind.

There was breathless fascination in the experience that drew her into a pleasantly unguarded state, an odd euphoria. She'd heard the term "rapture of the deep" and wondered if she might be experiencing "rapture of the kiss." Not a bad way to go, she decided, relishing this new, unforeseen facet of what a kiss could do. Without any thought for the consequences, she clutched his broad torso and held fast, her lips parting freely, craving more.

She knew a wild surge of pleasure as his mouth opened in answer to her silent urging, and his tongue began a languid quest, meeting the slick smoothness of her teeth. While he penetrated deeper, exploring the moist recesses of her mouth, she became aware of a new hunger—a hunger that was hot, and foretold of imminent, total surrender.

Sheer terror welled up inside her at the realization. *No!* her mind cried. *Not this man! Not another type A. Will you never learn, Jess? He'll smother you, take away the person you are, try to mold you into his image of what you should be. No! Run, you demented, weak, crazy woman!*

She began to tremble in his arms, tried to protest, but her voice wouldn't come, wouldn't aid in her escape. His hands were at her waist, drawing her closer to him, more intimately against his exhilarating hardness. She could feel his arousal, and knew that he was no mere machine. He was a complete, fully functioning man— with all the appropriate human needs and desires.

Feeling helpless, she whimpered forlornly, and pushed as fiercely as her flagging strength would allow. Surprisingly, she found herself released, free to run. Dazed by the depth of her reaction to his kiss, she stumbled away until she felt the blessed support of the tree trunk. Propped against its solidness, she swept a hand through her hair, pointedly avoiding his eyes. "I— That was uncalled-for," she croaked.

There was no sound, no apology, and she peeked up to judge his expression. His eyes were hooded, his lips pursed. She could read nothing of his thoughts.

"I—I said," she began again, then had to clear her passion-swollen throat. "I said that was uncalled-for."

He turned away. "I heard you."

As he picked up the stick he'd dropped earlier, she demanded, "Is that all? No apology? No explanation? Just 'I heard you'?"

He shifted to look down at her. "You were getting hysterical giving that type *A* speech. I didn't want to slap you, so I kissed you to calm you down."

She didn't know what she'd wanted him to say, but it certainly hadn't been that. Her cheeks fiery, she snapped, "Oh? Do your kisses usually send women into a coma?"

He considered her in the darkness. Along with the biting, tart smell of dead leaves and the cool hint of pine, she detected his scent on the breeze—or was it on her, now? Wincing, she tried not to breathe, or at least not to be so aware of his unique scent. It was too stimulating, too reminiscent of her near surrender moments ago.

"I'm sorry about your parents and your husband, Jess," he said at last. "I'm sorry I remind you of them. I'm also sorry I kissed you. I suppose I've been working too much, and I wasn't thinking clearly."

"Oh?" she blurted, irritated that he was casting off the kiss so casually. A mental aberration, nothing more! *How gallant!* "Well, don't worry, Mr. Brand. It's totally forgotten." She'd told several lies tonight, but none as big as that one. Swooping down to grab up her fallen stick, she glared at her wrist, provoked that she couldn't see her watch, and unsure why that bothered her so.

As she fumbled with her coat sleeve, Lucas said, "It's eleven-thirty."

"Another half hour." It came out in a woebegone moan, as though she was remarking on some unending medieval torture.

"I won't attack you again, if that's what you're worried about," he said gruffly.

"You bet you won't," she retorted. "If I want to be any calmer I'll smack myself with this stick until I lapse into unconsciousness. I won't be needing any further 'calming' from you!"

"You do wonders for a man's ego."

"Check my job description. It doesn't include ego stroking—"

A loud wail split the quiet, and Jess cried, "Oh, no! Not again!"

Lucas had struck off at a run. "This one sounds serious," he called back.

Her heart hammering with alarm, she hurried after him, clutching her stick like a bat. "What—do you think it is?" she panted.

"Hell if I know."

There was another scream, filled with terror.

Jess's stomach clenched. "You said wild dogs sometimes—"

"I don't know," he cut in, then came to such an abrupt halt she almost slammed into his back.

"Are you okay?" he asked.

Jess detected a familiar smell as she peered around Lucas to see what was going on. Suzy was cowering behind Larry Tenkiller. Jack was on his knees, petting a scrawny blond mutt that was giving off the all-too-familiar bouquet of *eau de* polecat.

"Get it away!" Suzy screamed. Get it away! It'll bite me!"

"It doesn't care about you," Jack groused. "It wants to be friends. Can't you see it's licking my hand, dummy?"

"It smells like—*totally gross.*"

"That's because it's been attacked by the skunks, too," Jack said, sounding put out.

"Duh," Moses quipped. "So tell us some jive we don't know, man."

"Are you people okay?" Jess ventured at last, stepping out from behind Lucas's broad back. "Did anybody get bitten?"

"Naw," Jack said, standing. "Poor dog stinks."

Lucas chuckled darkly. "There's a news flash."

"We got any more tomato juice?" Jack asked, looking as though he didn't expect much help with the stray.

"Why?" asked Lucas. "You want to bathe that mutt?"

Jack shrugged. "He stinks."

Lucas was frowning. Jess knew it wasn't her place to give Jack permission. It was Lucas's house, Lucas's tomato juice. Even so, she held on to a ray of hope.

"If you want to do the work, there's a big sink in the laundry room with a flexible shower head. Have Maxim get you what you need."

"Huh?" Jack said, looking like he doubted his own hearing.

Jess smiled, and her heart went out to Lucas. These unexpected flashes of altruism startled her and pulled at her heart. She had no idea what had possessed him to be this giving—allowing yet another stinking creature into his pristine home. Maybe he'd had a mutt he'd loved once. Maybe he'd wanted a dog and never been able to have one.

"You go on back to the house now, Jack," she said. "Wash the dog if you want."

He looked at her with an expression that was almost affectionate, except for the mistrust that seemed to permanently hover in his eyes. Without another word, he patted the dog's head and commanded gently, "Come on, boy," then headed off at a gallop.

"Whew," Suzy said, coming out from behind Larry. "I hate that stink! That Jack's crazy."

"I think it's cool," Annie insisted. "People who like dogs can't be all bad. Maybe Jack isn't such a total armpit."

"Well," Jess said, "now that *that* crisis is over, how's the hunt going?"

There was a communal moan. "Not so hot," Larry admitted.

Suzy laughed. "Yeah, Mr. Tracker's been a ton of help."

"Oh, *stuff it!*" Larry bellyached. "With you griping and whining about every little sound, thinking it was a bear or a rabid bat, how could we keep quiet enough to attract anything but smelly dogs!"

Jess pretended to check her watch. "It's time we started back. Maybe the other team won't have caught anything either."

"No kiddin'," Moses sneered. "With that duck, Molly Roberts, they'll catch nothin' but *ugly*. And I mean *butt* with two *t*s."

"You're the butt with two *t*s," Suzy snapped. "So Molly's shy and skinny and wears glasses. You're sleazy, skinny and you got a butt-ugly attitude. *Big* flippin' difference."

Moses opened his mouth to retort, but Jess broke in, "Okay, enough character assassination for now." Taking one of Larry's and one of Moses' hands, she steered them in the direction of the house. "Let's head back and see how team two did."

Out of the corner of her eye she saw Suzy and Annie each grab one of Lucas's hands and begin to tug him forward. Unable to stop herself, she peeked at the man's shadowed face. He was looking at her with a smug half grin—almost as though he thought she might be envious. How egotistical and idiotic of him! How utterly ridiculous! She sniffled huffily and turned away, demonstrating how little she cared that a few fourteen-year-old girls thought he was a "totally hot babe."

It was a shame, however, that the imp in her brain kept tormenting, *A totally hot babe—with haunting, tender kisses. . . .*

"ARE THERE REALLY ANY fish?" asked Larry Tenkiller. "Or is this another one of your fake snipe-hunt deals?"

Jess laughed. "I promise there are fish." She sniffed the crisp morning air and smiled. "At least there'd better be, 'cause we're supposed to eat our catch for lunch."

"Gross," Suzy chimed in. "Slimy, wiggly fish—with eyes? We have to eat them?"

Jess fingered a blond curl that had fallen over the girl's eye. "Believe me, when you smell them cooking, you'll change your mind."

Out of the corner of her eye, she saw Jack off by himself as usual, but with a hairy companion. The stray mongrel he'd taken back and bathed in tomato juice last night was prancing and playing around him as if the frowning young man was now the dog's own private property. Jess smiled. She'd heard through the very reliable teenage grapevine that, once everyone was in bed, Jack had sneaked down to the laundry room where the dog had been housed for the night, and had led him quietly upstairs to sleep on his bed.

Jack needed a friend badly, and it looked as though this dog might be just the catalyst to get the boy to begin to open up. Jess hoped so. And she also hoped Lucas would never hear of the late-night dog visit to the bedroom. She wasn't sure he'd take kindly to having hair-shedding beasts in his house.

She surveyed the group of young people, straggling out along the route to the wooded area where they were going to lounge around fishing, after gathering wood and rocks for the campfires. Maybe later there'd be a game of touch football. The weather was cooperating beautifully. Low sixties and sunny. Made to order for outside activities. Gorgeous day. Gorgeous weather.

The only blot on the excursion was the usual one— *Lucas Brand*. Everyone else was carrying fishing gear, but Lucas was toting his laptop computer. During the conference call this morning with Sol and Fletch, it had been decided that they'd all, independently, check the raw data for a program error.

So, while the kids were fishing, he'd physically be there, as required, but he'd be about as accessible, friendly and helpful as the Big Dipper constellation! "Big dip," she muttered.

"Talking to me?" he asked, and she jumped, not realizing he'd sneaked up behind her.

She glared at him. "No! And I won't be speaking to you as long as you're carrying around that little dingus."

He grinned wickedly. "Don't insult something you've never seen."

She frowned, then realized what he meant. "I said *dingus*, meaning thing—er—object . . ." She blanched.

It wasn't getting much better. *"Computer!"* she fairly shouted.

He lifted a brow as though that had never occurred to him. "You know, a good grasp of the language is invaluable. It can keep you out of trouble."

"You know, Lucas, you have a rare sense of humor," she gritted. "I hope they find the cure soon."

"Don't sell your little band of misfits short," he warned ominously. "They could cure most bouts of good humor. And as for my dingus, let's not get started on that subject again. Let's just agree to disagree. You know I have a deadline."

"Mr. Niceguy?" someone asked in a faint little voice.

Both Jess and Lucas turned to see Molly Roberts standing there, her slight frame dwarfed by the long fishing pole resting on her shoulder. Her hazel eyes were big and worried-looking behind her thick glasses, and her mouth was pinched in distress. The stocking cap over her short, stringy brown hair, made her look like a frail little boy.

"Yes, Molly," Jess replied. Though Molly hadn't been addressed, she wanted to protect the girl's feelings if Lucas didn't remember her name.

Molly glanced from Lucas to Jess, then back to Lucas. "I—I was just wondering what happened to your eye?"

Jess blanched. Though only his lid had turned blue, and the resulting bruise wasn't too bad, she felt rotten and guilty about having hit him last night.

Lucas shrugged and smiled at the girl. "I ran into something in the dark," he answered simply.

"Does it hurt?" Molly asked. Jess knew the girl wanted to become a nurse one day, and in Jess's opinion she'd be a wonderful addition to a caring profession.

"Only hurts when I shave," he teased.

Molly blinked, then a slow smile blossomed on her thin lips. "You're kidding me."

"Maybe a little around the edges," he admitted.

"I think it's gonna be okay," Molly offered. "But next time put ice on it right away. Helps it not be so purple."

Lucas gave her a serious I'm-paying-attention look and nodded. "Check. Ice right away. Thanks."

Molly's cheeks became two glowing maroon dots on her pale skin. "It's nothing. I mean, like—I mean . . ." She motioned broadly with a delicate hand. "Well— you're being so neat and cool with us. Me trying to help isn't that big a deal. . . ." Her cheeks flushed even brighter, in her embarrassment. That had probably been the longest speech she'd ever uttered.

Lucas frowned, seeming daunted for the first time since Jess had met the man. "It's nothing, Molly. Nothing," he muttered.

"Hey, Molly!" Suzy shouted. "Quit brownnosing Mr. Niceguy. Come over here and show Annie how you can wiggle your ears one at a time. She thinks I'm lying."

Molly gave Lucas one last, bashful grin and trotted off.

Lucas and Jess strolled along side by side. The silence between them was strained, but the exuberant kids dashing about didn't seem to notice the tension.

"Well, well," she finally said. "Did I see Mr. One-Hundred-Million-Dollar Project feel a twinge of guilt back there? Is it, maybe, a little hard to be idolized and know you don't deserve it?"

He scowled down at her. "I'm here, aren't I?"

She sniffed with contempt. "Yes. And a bureau is *in* a bedroom, but it'd better not try to pass itself off as a mattress!"

"That's probably very Freudian, but I'll let it go," he muttered.

She found herself flushing. "Big of you," she retorted, wondering where that particular bedroom image had come from.

SEVERAL HOURS LATER, Jess's irritation at Lucas lessened, especially when he left his computer to help the squeamish amateurs in their group clean their catch of rainbow trout. Unfortunately for her, the kids had scattered, and several had opted for the rowboat. The Goodalls had gone after the kids who'd run off along the south bank, the Kornblums had trekked off to round up stragglers to the north. It seemed that, once again, Jess had been paired with Lucas.

She supposed it made sense to the married folks that she'd join up with the other single on the retreat. But she was annoyed and agitated—especially after her speech last night, and Lucas's gentle kiss. Still, after avoiding him as much as possible all morning, she began to realize that she'd had help—*actual help*—teaching the kids to clean and cook their fish. He'd turned out to be more talented at it than she was. After tasting his efforts, she had to admit she'd never eaten better fried fish, not even in a restaurant.

Now pleasantly full of lunch, some in the group lazed around, a couple tossed a football, and Moses and Larry were back in the rowboat, fishing.

Jess glanced at Lucas. He'd picked up the computer again. Though she was about ten feet away, she craned her head around to see what was on the screen. You'd think it was a parade of leggy models, the way he was glued to it! But no. Long lines of figures and symbols were marching rapidly down the screen. They made no sense to her, but apparently Lucas was interpreting their correctness and moving on with something close to lightning speed. He must have quite an excellent mind, she decided, and tried not to dwell on the fact that his kisses, too, were quite excellent.

Jess was irritated, and not all of her irritation was directed at Lucas. She was irritated with herself for her unruly turn of mind of late. Not caring to analyze it, she opted instead for trying to get Lucas more involved in the retreat—the Mr. Niceguy program *not* the computer program. She cleared her throat meaningfully, attracting his narrowed gaze. Indicating his computer screen with a nod, she called, "About done?"

He gave her a look that said something along the lines of, *Do pigs fly?*

She didn't allow his insinuated sarcasm to intimidate her and forged on, "I was just wondering where you learned to clean and cook fish."

There was suddenly a tinge of sadness in his eyes. He glanced away, and stared off into space.

"My grandmother and I lived simply," he said after a moment. "Sometimes what we caught was all we had to eat."

Jess absorbed this, looking down at her clasped hands, then ventured, "What happened to your folks?"

He turned to gauge her, his expression opening into a questioning grin. There was no trace of humor in his eyes, though. "I can't imagine why you'd care. But, my folks had the same problem as Molly's. They got into drugs. In and out of rehab. Ultimately, I don't know."

She was saddened for him, but surprised that he knew about the shy little girl with the worried hazel eyes. "How did you know about Molly's background?"

He shrugged. "You gave me those profiles."

"You read them?" She asked, increduous.

He closed his computer and set it aside. "They were short."

The darned guy was surprising her again. He obviously was reluctant to do this retreat, with his laptop ever-present, his cigarette-case-size phone ringing every fifteen minutes, and his habitual glancing down at his wristwatch. But to give credit where it was due, what Lucas had done, he'd done well. She didn't seem to be able to find much fault with him right this minute. "Molly likes you a lot, you know," Jess murmured, feeling she owed him that much. "They all do."

He stared out across the water at Moses and Larry's, horseplay in the rowboat. "So where are Molly's folks?"

The kids were far enough away not to have heard their conversation so far, but Jess got up and moved over to sit down beside him—not quite close enough to touch, but close enough to catch his scent. She crossed her legs, Indian-style. "Didn't want to shout this," she said, explaining away her motive for getting closer. "Molly's folks are dead. And she didn't have any grandmother to take her in. Been in foster care for five years."

"I know about the foster homes," he reminded her. "By the way, I knew Molly's name this morning when you ran interference for me. For future reference, I know all their names. I have one of those photographic memories."

"Oh," she said, an embarrassed smile quivering on her lips. "I didn't know about that." Spying Larry scooping up water and splashing Moses with it, she shouted, "Hey, cut that out, you guys!"

"Where are their life jackets?" Lucas asked.

Both boys had turned to grin at her and ignored the command completely. Jess frowned. "Life jackets? I—I'm sure they had them on when they went out." Unease prickled along her spine. "Darned kids. Think they're invincible."

Leaping up, she shouted, "And put your life jackets back on! Now, I *mean*—" Her warning was cut short when Moses, in an attempt to avoid another faceful of cold water, jumped up, then lost his balance. Jess gaped as the teenager, in macabre slow motion, pitched backward over the side of the boat into the frigid water.

"*Oh my Lord!*" Jess wailed. She flung off her coat as she streaked toward the lake, then with a shallow, running dive, hurled herself into the drink. When she came up, she fought off the shock of the icy water, shouting toward a group of kids who had gathered on the shore. "Throw the *cooler!* Throw something to help him float!"

As she swam toward Moses, who was not the world's best swimmer, she heard a plop. Someone had thrown something. She turned to see what it was, and was startled to see Lucas's computer begin to sink beneath the surface. Shocked, her gaze darted toward shore. Lucas looked angry enough to commit murder.

It didn't surprise her much when he hurriedly pulled off his boots, ducked out of his wool turtleneck, and dived in. His computer was probably too valuable to lose without a fight, though she would have thought that being dunked in a lake would have ruined it.

Hearing Moses' strangled shout, she turned back to her rescue attempt. He was too far out to reach with anything from shore. "Grab the boat," she cried, spitting water. "Larry, put out an oar to him!"

She continued shouting instructions and encouragement between inhaling mouthfuls of water. Her throat was raw, her lungs half flooded, and she was barely a third of the way there. Why did they look like they were getting farther and farther away? Her arms ached but she struggled on, weighed down by her sweater and her hiking boots. She wasn't the world's best swimmer, either, especially dragged down by soaked clothing that felt like a twenty-ton block of cement.

She didn't relish dying this way. But worse, she couldn't bear the idea of Moses dying on a retreat that was supposed to have been a reward for his initiative and hard work. She made a vow to heaven. People like her father and mother, like her ex and Lucas Brand, could make her feel as mediocre as they wanted, make her feel as lousy and unsuccessful as they pleased, she would pay whatever price Providence required of her—but, *Please, please,* she prayed, *let me reach Moses in time!*

8

AS JESS STRUGGLED toward Moses, coughing and sputtering, she heard a male voice shout, "When I shove you up, grab the opposite side of the boat and swing a leg over."

She wiped water from her eyes, and squinted. Lucas had reached the rowboat ahead of her. He shouted again. "Larry, get low in the center, and grab Moses' arm when he comes up over the side."

Jess began to dog-paddle, watching in confusion. What was Lucas doing out there? Why wasn't he saving his computer?

He disappeared beneath the surface. After another few seconds she saw a flailing Moses catapulted up and out of the water. He belly flopped over the side of the boat, and immediately swung a leg up and over the gunwale. Larry grabbed Moses by his soggy jacket and hauled him, gagging and spitting, into the bottom of the rowboat.

Before Jess realized he had moved away from the boat, Lucas was beside her, grasping her by the upper arm. "Let's get you back to shore," he said, sounding slightly winded. Jess cast one last glance at the boat. Larry, looking wretched and guilt-ridden, was rowing for all he was worth. Moses' nose was the only part of him visible above the gunwale, for he was slumped backward, exhausted, his head lolling on the seat.

She shifted her attention back to Lucas, and gasped, "You—you jumped in to save Moses?"

He seemed surprised by her question. "Why else?"

"I—I thought you were—uh—saving your computer. . . ."

He scowled. "You have quite an opinion of me, don't you?"

She opened her mouth, but inhaled more water and choked.

"You okay?" Lucas asked. Though his tone was edged with resentment, she saw a shadow of concern in his eyes.

"I—I'm—" She broke off as more water sloshed into her mouth, bringing on a gut-wrenching fit of coughing.

Lucas began tugging her toward shore, and she felt humiliation clench her stomach. Another failure. Another type *A* deciding she needed rescuing, deciding she couldn't manage on her own. "Lu—Lucas," she spat out between gasps for air. "*Please*. let go of my arm. I—I'm not drowning. . . ."

He didn't oblige her at first, accusing, "You're doing a pretty good imitation of it."

She was treading water in the world's heaviest boots, peering at him between strands of water-soaked hair. "Please . . ." she moaned hoarsely. "Don't treat me like a child."

"I'm not trying to dominate or control you, Jess. I'm trying to help."

"I know, I know. I appreciate it, really," she wheezed, then added, almost begging, "*Please—let go* . . ."

His frown told her of his reluctance, but he finally let go. Without a word, they swam back toward shore. Jess knew he was slowing his pace to match hers, but now it wasn't quite so obvious she was the less capable of the two.

She knew she was acting irrationally, being so touchy about not wanting his help. Especially after the vow she'd just made to heaven that she would endure any humiliation if Moses' life was spared. But she'd spent so many years receiving unsolicited "help" from people who thought what they were doing was for her own good, it was practically impossible to endure any, so-called help these days—even, apparently, when her life was at stake.

As they neared shore, the rowboat caught up and wedged itself between them. Its oars dipped and rose frantically, gouging out explosive showers of water, as Larry did his inept best to get Moses to land. Jess could hear Larry's labored breathing as he rowed. Though she couldn't see his face, she could tell he was worried for his friend's health, and upset by what his recklessness had caused.

When the boat bumped the shore, Lucas scrambled onto the grass and helped Moses out. Jess noticed that he ignored her as she hauled herself weakly from the frigid water. She tottered to the boat as Larry hopped out to help Lucas with Moses. She grabbed the piece of rope that was used to tie it to the dock and wrapped it around a sapling that grew near the water's edge. Then, hardly able to support her own weight, she stumbled over to retrieve her coat, her ruined shoes squishing loudly as she went.

The other kids in their group had gathered around Lucas as he pulled on his dry sweater and boots. Shuddering, Jess huddled in her parka, which did little to ward off the cold. She noticed that Molly was sobbing, and reached out an arm to comfort her. "Everything's okay, honey," she soothed. "Don't worry."

The girl looked up, her face ghostly pale. "But—but I didn't know you said 'cooler.' I thought you said 'computer,'" she wailed. "I thought it could float or something." She gulped. "I'm sorry, I threw it—" Her mournful apology was interrupted as she burst into sobs and buried her face in her hands.

So that's how the computer got into the lake, Jess mused sadly. *Poor Molly.* Hugging the quaking girl, she whispered, "You thought you were doing right. And you acted quickly." She turned to Lucas. "Mr. Niceguy doesn't blame you," she assured Molly, casting a threatening look at Lucas that said, *You hurt this child's feelings and I'll have your heart!*

He met her gaze, and in a split second his anger and frustration about the thousands of dollars' worth of computer hardware that had been lost and the multi-million-dollar contract that was slipping rapidly out of his grasp was silently communicated.

Then Lucas's hard glance shifted away from Jess and settled on Molly, her face buried in her hands, her thin shoulders quaking. His expression softened slightly with what might have been pity. "It wasn't your fault, Molly," he said. "*I* thought she said, 'Throw *cat litter.*' Figured she was out of her head from the cold, so I jumped in."

Molly looked up and blinked her big, liquid eyes at him. Several of the kids laughed at his unexpectedly humorous remark. Jess simply stared.

"I'll—pay you back," Molly whispered brokenly.

He shrugged. "Tell you what," he suggested. "You take my next turn at peeling potatoes and we'll call it even."

Molly swallowed several times, then the beginnings of a grateful smile quirked her lips. "I'll peel all your potatoes from now on, Mr. Niceguy," she offered.

He grinned at her and Jess felt the appeal of it radiate through her frozen core, kindling a new warmth within her. "Just once is fine," he said, then turned back to Jess. "We'd better get Moses to the house to dry off," he reminded, more brusquely.

"Yes—I suppose we had," she agreed, her voice quivery with cold and fatigue, and something more. Perhaps it was gratitude for what he'd done for Molly. Or, maybe it had been his gentle smile, reminding her of the unexpected sweetness of his kiss last night. In spite of her resolve not to dwell on it, the memory came back to haunt her, robbing her of any peace of mind.

Larry stripped off his coat and put it over Moses' shoulders, muttering in a strained tone, "I'll run on ahead and tell 'em to get some blankets ready."

Lucas nodded. "Good idea. We'll be right there."

Bernie came up puffing and took charge of the remaining group, but Jess hardly noticed. Her consciousness was focused on Lucas, who had slung a protective arm about Moses' quaking shoulders to help him forward.

She guessed he was starting to relate to this boy—to all of these kids. Somehow, slowly, he was remembering how it had been for him, and he was opening up. Not by much, yet. But that one, spontaneous movement to try to warm Moses himself, despite his own obvious discomfort, was certainly telling.

She felt a stirring of fondness for the man. During the past twenty-four hours, Jess had been witness to the fact that he wasn't a man devoid of passions. His were simply directed in areas other than personal relationships—a tragedy, for he could probably be a loving, caring man. Exactly what she needed most in her life. But, getting involved with Lucas Brand would never do. *Never.* He had no intention of redirecting his passions away from making money toward making people happy. Unfortunately for Jess, however, those dark eyes beckoned, beckoned....

But she'd *never* be so stupid as to fall for another type A man again. Especially not the very man who'd been partly responsible for the breakup of both her parents' and her own marriage! She's be a crazy, self-destructive idiot if she allowed such a thing.

The trio headed toward the house, Jess trailing tensely a few paces back. She watched her tall, drenched host from under her lashes, hating the fact that she was so drawn to him. His jeans were plastered to his legs, showing off every taut male muscle of his hips and thighs. Focusing on the back of his dark head, she wondered what was in his mind. He'd been gracious to Molly, and Jess was grateful for that. At least he wasn't a man who humiliated children. Or grown women, for that matter. He'd certainly left her alone when she'd asked—begged, she amended, smarting inwardly as she recalled the humbling scene in the lake.

She wondered if he was angry that she'd rejected his help. Or had his abandonment when she'd gotten out of the water been his way of allowing her to be the strong, independent woman she wanted to be?

"You're pretty quiet back there," Lucas called, slowing his pace to allow her to catch up with them.

She was pleased to suddenly be included. Lucas and Moses had been talking, but embroiled in her own mental turmoil, she hadn't heard what they'd said. Hurrying forward, she asked, "How are you doing, Moses?"

He looked at her for a minute, then cast a dejected gaze at the ground. "I'm gonna get k-k-kicked out on my butt, ain't I?" he grumbled through chattering teeth.

She frowned at him. "Of course not." Taking his hand in a reassuring gesture, she said, "Actually, you're going to get some dry clothes and some hot chocolate."

He peered over at her. "Ain't you ticked?"

She squeezed his fingers. "I've been ticked worse."

"No jive?" he asked, sounding incredulous. "I don't have t-to go home?"

She shook her head. "Hey, Moses, we all make mistakes. Next time, you'll remember to wear your life jacket. Okay?"

He snorted. "Won't be no next time this trip, man. That water's cold as a witch's b-butt."

Lucas chuckled. "I couldn't have put it better myself."

Once they'd handed the quaking teenager over to a couple of servants who wrapped him in a towel and were escorting him to a hot bath, Jess turned to Lucas and whispered, "Cat litter?" She found herself breaking into a smile at the craziness of his response earlier to Molly.

He lifted a derisive brow. "You want poetry, get Robert Frost. That look of yours didn't give me much time to come up with a good lie."

She gathered the wool blanket that enveloped her more tightly about her shoulders as she and Lucas headed up the back stairs to hot baths of their own. Her smile faded. "How bad was it—I mean, what you lost?"

He exhaled tiredly. "The phone that fell out of my pocket was no great loss. And, I've got the Takahashi program here on hard disk. Mainly I lost a damn fine computer and time I can't afford to lose."

As they reached the second-floor landing where Lucas's room was, she took hold of his hand. "Lucas—" she began tentatively, "today, you were truly the Mr. Niceguy I'd hoped for. Thanks."

He turned on her sharply. His dark eyes narrowed as they stared at her hand holding his. Though he had donned that familiar air of isolation, Jess wasn't intimidated by it, now. She'd discovered new facets of Lucas Brand. Like the way he could smile at a frightened little girl and ease her fears, or fling a fatherly arm about a quaking boy to warm and comfort him. And most important of all, she'd felt the gentleness of his kiss. Bravely, she smiled in the face of his aloof manner, holding tightly to his fingers. "Maybe Mr. Roxbury knew what he was doing after all," she whispered.

His eyes flashed a warning, but she was no longer frightened by that look. Suddenly embarrassed by her uncharacteristic boldness, she slid her fingers from his. "I'm—I'm truly grateful," she offered unsteadily.

"Are you talking about what I did for Molly, or in the water with you?"

She flushed. "Both—I suppose."

He was wearing his blank computer-screen stare, and she couldn't begin to guess his thoughts. "Don't be grateful to me," he cautioned. "Just because I'm not a beast who makes little girls cry, and because I let you struggle to shore half drowned, doesn't make me any more your Mr. Niceguy than I was the day we met." He turned away, summarily dismissing her with his abrupt departure.

She watched him stalk off, sensing that he was angrier with himself than with her. Both of them knew he'd gone farther today than he'd probably ever expected he would toward being what Mr. Roxbury wanted in his substitute Mr. Niceguy.

Lucas's attitude had mellowed toward the kids, toward the project. Why couldn't he concede that he owned a heart, and could even use it when called upon? *Darn his stubborn hide!*

Shaking her head, she trudged on up the stairs to the third floor, weary all the way to the ends of her dripping hair. "Why are you so afraid to care about people, Lucas?" she murmured sadly.

THE KIDS WERE IN THE great room, watching a film the Goodalls had rented for them. Tonight was to be a relaxing evening after a long, active day. Since Lucas's presence wasn't required during the screening, he'd retired to his computer room to go over his program in peace.

Whatever the movie was, it must have been funny, because every so often he could hear the young people burst out laughing. He frowned, realizing his mind wasn't on the scrolling display of figures on the computer screen. With a keystroke, he moved the display back and restarted it, only to be immediately distracted. "Damn it to hell," he muttered and began the scrolling over again.

The phone rang, and he picked up the receiver. "Brand, here," he barked.

"This is Fletch. Just got word that Cybertronics has dropped out of the race."

Lucas was surprised by the news. Cybertronics was one of their strongest competitors for the Takahashi contract. "Did you hear why?" he asked.

"Can't conquer the cordless glove—uh . . ." Fletch halted, wisely not voicing his thought.

"Don't you dare say, *either*," Lucas warned. "We're going to find the glitch in the program and get this deal if it's the last thing we do."

"Uh, right," Fletch said. "You find anything on your end?"

"No. I'm working on it now." Deciding not to tell Fletch the absurd story about how his computer got thrown into the lake, he just said, "Had a problem with my XJ 9000 this morning. What about you and Sol? Find anything in the sensor system?"

"*Nada*, but we're staying with it."

"Check with me before you go home."

"Home?" Fletch scoffed. "I'm not familiar with the word."

"Hilarious," Lucas said tonelessly, then hung up.

As he moved to reset his computer, he paused, cursed and sagged back wearily. Closing his eyes, he did something he rarely ever did—let his mind wander. Irritated, but knowing he wasn't getting any work done, he decided he might as well get this thing sorted out in his mind and file it away so he could get on with his life, and his work. What difference would fifteen lousy minutes make?

Why in hell had he kissed Jess Glen last night? The question had gnawed at him all day. And, if he were to be honest, it had cost him what little sleep he might have had when he'd finally given in to exhaustion around four in the morning, and had fallen into bed.

Maybe his lapse had been due partly to nostalgia. He hadn't gone walking in that part of the woods since— well, for years. It had brought back memories of happier times. That's probably why he'd lingered with Jess instead of going back to the house. Damn, it had been eerie to walk there. To be so near his . . .

He ran a restless hand through his hair, cursed again and decided to face the fact that it hadn't been *only* that. Not simple nostalgia. It had been Jess, too. That flustered, brave little speech had given him new insight into why she was the way she was, why she automatically disliked men like him and was nervous when he was around.

She'd been bossed and badgered a lot in her life, and she was sick of it. He could see now why she wanted desperately to be a person in her own right—not one who someone else was molding like sculptor's clay, but her own person. People in her past had made her terribly vulnerable, damn them. She'd proved *that* today when she would rather have drowned than accept his help and maybe get a little ribbing. When she'd pleaded with him, choking and coughing, her frightened eyes bright with tears, he'd felt like kissing her again, right there in front of God and everyone.

What was it about her that made him want to take her in his arms and protect her? That was the last thing she wanted from him—or from anyone. She wanted respect and fair treatment, and he didn't blame her, didn't fault her. Unexpectedly, last night he'd felt her pain, witnessed her shattered confidence, and it had touched something inside him.

He'd made an effort over the years to empty himself of emotions and sentiment. That's why the kiss had surprised him so. It had shocked her, but it had blown him away. He hadn't kissed a woman out of simple caring in a lot of years; had never expected or wanted to, again. Yet, he'd felt a stirring last night, and had acted on it. Not the brightest idea he'd had lately, but it had been too strong to ignore.

It had been some sort of twisted, crazy urge to help, he guessed—no doubt due to his fatigue and the lack of female companionship since he'd begun this damned Takahashi thing a month ago. He'd regretted his actions immediately, but hadn't been able to forget how perfectly attuned their kiss had been, how damned quickly and thoroughly the whisper-light touch of their lips had become wildly hungry; and that memory rode him hard.

Over the years, he'd learned to distance himself from pain, both his own and other people's. Since his divorce, he'd made it a practice—no, a *strict policy*—not to get involved. Especially with women who wore their hearts on their sleeves and lived by their emotions—like Jess.

Why, then, was he suddenly ambivalent about his strict policy of noninvolvement? What was it about her that made him want to punch somebody? Her father, maybe? Or her ass of an ex-husband? Why did he want to shout, "Leave the woman alone. She's damned pushy enough the way she is!"

He almost smiled at that. For a woman who thought she was a failure, she'd gotten him to do things for her he'd never have done for anyone else. Damned honest gray eyes of hers. He snorted derisively. He knew she wasn't manipulative. He knew she'd tried her damnedest to be, but it just wasn't her nature. Still, in her own decent, scrupulous way, she'd handled him like a pro. He was strangely ambivalent about that, too. Sometimes her directness irritated the fire out of him, and other times, like when she was sputtering out her "You bother me" speech last night, it sent a stab of feeling through him that he couldn't quite identify—and couldn't quite ignore.

As he rocked back in his swivel chair, listening to the faint squeak of its hinges, he found himself fantasizing about making love to her. She was so caring and vulnerable with the kids, and so guarded with him. What would it be like, he wondered, to see her flushed with passion, gasping and moaning softly in his arms? Beautifully naked, her silky skin wet and pulsing against his. He gritted his teeth, crushing the dangerous image. But another emerged in its place, just as haunting, and every bit as dangerous: the image of Jess today, when she'd shocked him by taking his fingers in hers.

He'd resisted squeezing back, had balked at the compliment and the intimacy. He fisted the hand she'd held so tightly. He *wasn't* Mr. Niceguy, *dammit*. Wasn't the generous soul old Roxbury was, and he didn't want to care to deceive the woman who was looking at him with a new, almost-admiring expression. He'd backed off, growled at her. Rejected her approval.

It was best that he had, he told himself. She was an open person by nature. Unfortunately, people who were supposed to have loved her had given her a lot of emotional scars. It was ironic, he mused. Both he and Jess were guarded in their own ways. She'd never had much affection in her life, or much approval. By working with these kids, she was getting both, at last.

Because Lucas had known affection, but had lost it suddenly and cruelly, he no longer sought it. He rejected it, and didn't give a damn about anyone's approval. They were an interesting twosome, he and Jess Glen. Very different, but ironically alike.

Though the kiss they'd shared had proved they were highly compatible sexually, pulling her into bed would be a mistake. It might do his ego some momentary good, but it would only make her more guarded and inhibited when the affair ended. He didn't want to add to her hurts, and offering uncommitted sex to a woman who wanted affection and emotional attachment would be underhanded and sleazy.

He knew he had to steer clear. But the memory of the kiss nagged, driving him crazy. *Dammit!* He jerked forward and switched on the diagnostics. Enough time had been wasted dwelling on that idiotic kiss. It was time he moved on.

"Hey, man," came a voice from behind him. Swiveling around in his chair, he saw Molly and Moses standing just inside the door. The thin girl, her hair pulled back into a runty ponytail, was carrying a plate with what looked like a sandwich on it. Moses held a steaming mug.

Lucas sat forward, frowning, but not particularly irritated by the interruption. Maybe a break was a good idea. "What can I do for you two?"

They were looking around the room, clearly in awe of the advanced technology they were seeing. "*Shi*— uh—" Moses began, then amended, "Shoot, man, you know how to work all this stuff?"

Lucas raked an impatient gaze over the computer equipment. "The board of directors thinks so," he muttered.

"What is it you're doing?" asked Molly.

He shrugged. "Working on a Virtual Reality program for a pharmaceutical company in Japan." Lucas indicated the helmet sitting on the desktop to his left. "This is what we call an HMD, or head-mounted display. Through it we see a Virtual, or imaginary, world. And this—" he lifted the glove, barely able to keep the anger at the malfunctioning piece of junk from his voice "—is our cordless, force-feedback glove. It lets you feel an imaginary thing the way it would really feel. Say, an imaginary marshmallow that feels spongy, like a real marshmallow, or an imaginary rock that feels hard, like a real rock." He slipped on the silver glove and opened and closed his fingers in a clawlike maneuver. "This drug company wants a computer program that'll help them pick up molecules and move them around so they can improve medicines."

"But molecules are too small to move with your hand," Molly said, a confused frown puckering her forehead.

"That's true," Lucas agreed, giving the girl an approving nod. "So my job is to make imaginary molecules that are big enough to move with this glove, and to see through this helmet, so the computer can then work microscopic tools that do the same thing to the real molecules."

"No jive?" Moses exclaimed.

"No jive," Lucas echoed, pleased at the boy's interest. "The drug company hopes this new technology will help reduce the costs of products."

"Cool," Molly breathed. "You're almost like a saint to be working on something so wonderful."

Lucas halted in the act of taking off his glove, and shot her a startled glance. "I wouldn't say I'm very close to sainthood," he hedged, embarrassed by the young girl's admiration. "It's my business to come up with computer programs."

"But you do such awesome stuff, Mr. Niceguy," she objected passionately. "You're a *totally awesome* man."

He felt a prick of guilt as he turned away to finish removing the glove. "What is that you two brought?" he asked brusquely, anxious to change the subject.

"We, uh, thought you might be hungry," Molly offered, still sounding too impassioned for Lucas's peace of mind. He turned to stare somberly at her. She held out the plate, but did not move forward.

He realized now why neither of them had come any closer. To a fourteen-year-old, his equipment no doubt looked like the inside of an alien spacecraft. "I am a little hungry, at that," he admitted, feeling the weariness of the past several weeks lying heavily on his shoulders. "Thanks." He got up and indicated a table and four chairs in the corner near the door. "I'll eat over there."

Molly and Moses, hurrying along the far wall, beat him to the table and had set down his sandwich and mug by the time he got there. Lucas was surprised to see he'd been brought a cup of cocoa instead of coffee. "Looks good," he offered less gruffly, realizing how really hungry he was.

"Mrs. Glen thought you might be ready for something," Molly said, taking a step back, as though she still feared he might reach out and slug her for tossing his computer into the lake.

After seating himself, he ran a hand over his face, rubbing his eyes. "Tell her thanks," he said, tiredly. Then, looking at the boy, he asked, "How are you feeling, Moses?"

He shrugged. "Like a dumb-butt, but I ain't cold anymore." He elbowed Molly gently. "We both feel pretty stupid."

Molly bit her lower lip. "Yeah," she added shyly. "Spitball told me those little computers can cost a couple of thousand dollars—" She broke off suddenly, as tears flooded her eyes. The storm of emotion was so unexpected, Lucas was taken aback. He flinched, lowering the sandwich he'd been about to bite into.

"Hey—" He reached out and took her hand. "Cut that out," he cautioned gently. "We had a deal. You're peeling my potatoes remember?"

She sniffled. "But—I ruined an *expensive computer!*" she sobbed, brokenly.

She was right about that—except for one small detail. The XJ 9000 had cost fifteen thousand dollars, not two. Frowning at her distress, he squeezed her fingers. "Molly, I don't usually brag to women about my finances," he said, with a grin he hoped would charm her out of her tears, "but I'm filthy, stinking rich. I could toss one of those little toys in the lake every day if I wanted and still be able to afford cable TV." He squeezed her hand again, then let go, adding, "Besides, I have insurance for stuff like that. Won't cost me a dime."

She blinked, and sniffed. "You—you sure?"

"Would Mr. Niceguy lie?" he asked, ashamed at his use of the title he didn't feel worthy of. But he figured it was a label she'd have faith in, and he hoped it would get her mind off the damned computer.

Molly seemed to relax slightly. His reference to the damned Mr. Niceguy fraud he was perpetrating had done what he'd wanted it to. She swallowed and wiped her nose with the napkin she'd brought. "I—I made the sandwich," she said, her voice almost steady.

Moses added, "I made the cocoa. Larry's trying to say he's sorry by helpin' Jack wash that moron dog."

Lucas was confused. "What moron dog?"

"You know," Moses said, "the dumb one that chases skunks. He came home smellin' like shi—uh—smellin' gross, again."

Lucas shook his head. "Moron sounds like a good name for a dog who likes to chase skunks."

Molly giggled, and that surprised Lucas. She seemed to have bounced back quickly with his reassurance. "I'll tell Jack," she was saying. "It's nicer than most of the names he's been calling that mutt." Her big eyes were still glistening with liquid, but she seemed at peace, somehow. Lucas felt an odd gratification about that, then he caught himself and grunted at his slackening of control. "If you kids will excuse me, I have to get back to work."

"Right. No problem," Moses said, tugging on Molly's sleeve. "See ya tomorrow, man."

"Sure." He didn't look up as they left the room. After a minute he took a bite of the sandwich. Leftover meat loaf from the dinner the kids had concocted last night. He chewed, deciding it tasted pretty good. He hadn't had leftover meat loaf sandwiches since he was a kid. Eyeing the cocoa dubiously, he considered it. Odd how the world could grow colder, crueler, the economy could crumble, countries could wage wars all around the globe, but somehow, cocoa seemed to remain a quaint constant in his life. Somehow it wasn't just a drink; it invariably came to him as an offering of thanks or help or hope.

He scowled in contemplation. Once, he'd heard a quote—actually a question—that went something like, "Who knows where great things begin?" A long time ago, a great thing had begun for him when he'd been offered a simple cup of cocoa. He lifted the mug, staring at it. Though he wasn't crazy about the sweet taste, he took a swallow. It warmed him, and he felt curiously melancholy.

"I hope I'm not intruding." Jess's hesitant voice shattered his pensive mood and he glanced over to where she stood by the door. All the apprehension she'd ever harbored for him seemed to have returned to her face, and stiffened her stance. He found himself regretting that.

Though obviously she'd distanced herself emotionally from him since her attempt at friendship this afternoon, she *looked* much improved over the last time he'd seen her, dirt-caked and drenched. Her light-colored hair hung straight to her shoulders, and her wispy bangs half hid expressive gray eyes. Her features were earnest, though apprehensive. He wondered if she had any idea how lovely she was in her own quiet, insecure way.

She had a skittish, fawnlike beauty, especially when casually dressed in jeans and a sweater. She was softer this way than in those power suits she'd worn when they'd first met. Now he understood how out of place she'd felt in them, how she'd never really been herself, dressed for success. She didn't even like the power-dresser types. Preferred comfortable clothes and affectionate relationships, not boardrooms and techno-bull—any kind of bull, for that matter.

She was a caring, vulnerable person. He found himself warming to the idea of making love to her again, as the memory of their kiss raced through his mind with renewed vigor. But he squelched the thought along with the smile that had almost made it to his lips. "What is it?" he asked, purposefully gruff.

Her tentative smile faded and she gave him a mildly offended look as she approached the table. "Do you realize you have an exasperating habit of making people come to you?"

He scanned her skeptically. "I've been eating sitting down for a long time. I didn't know it was so daunting."

She flushed, disconcerted. "You're in a charming mood," she said, her voice edged with sarcasm. "Find your mistake yet?"

"No," he admitted gruffly, trying not to give a damn about her feelings. "What do you want?"

She pulled out a chair and sat down, her expression pained. "Okay. You want to play it this way, I can be grouchy, too." She planted her elbows on the table and laced her fingers below her chin. He had a feeling the move was to keep from tapping her nails nervously on the table. "How familiar are you with horses?" she asked.

"I've heard of them, but I've never made love to one. Is that all?"

"That's terribly charming, but not what I meant," she chided. "I meant, can you *ride?*"

"It's been a long time."

"Well, don't worry." She stood and assumed a pose every bit as dismissive as his had been, earlier that day. "I'm sure it'll come back to you. See you at eight sharp for a day of horseback riding."

"Or what?"

She gave him one of those stringent looks he'd gotten used to. They were more engaging than intimidating, and he fought an urge to tell her so.

"Or *this*, Mr. Niceguy," she warned, turning away. "If you *don't* show up, you're a dead man."

"I hope you realize murder can't solve all of life's little problems," he taunted.

"Maybe not," she retorted over her shoulder. "But it would sure put a dent in *mine.*"

Lucas sat back, watching the inviting sway of her hips as she marched away. A smile played on his lips in spite of himself.

9

JESS HAD NEVER RIDDEN a horse before becoming Mr. Roxbury's assistant. Every year at the retreat, she endured the agony of bouncing around in the saddle, getting bruised and battered pretending to be a cowgirl. And, though she was getting better, she was still no Dale Evans. "Whoa, Snowflake," she challenged, irritated that the horse had a mind of its own, and no matter how she tugged on the reins, she kept getting separated from the rest of the group.

Luckily, both Bertha and Bernie were excellent riders. And strangely enough, Lucas had turned out to be more than a glowering burden today. He rode well, maneuvered his horse like a man who'd done it before and done it well. He'd said he hadn't ridden in a long time, but he hadn't said he'd been extremely good at it.

She'd been too busy trying to keep from being scraped off her saddle under one low branch after another, or struggling to help one of the kids who were experiencing similar problems, to have any conversation with Lucas. But he was there, sitting on that horse as tall and broad-shouldered as John Wayne had ever been, chasing after straying horses and guiding them back into line. Except for her, of course. She was on her own, as far as he was concerned.

She supposed it was for the best. After all, she'd told him to leave her alone, and she wanted him to leave her alone. But right now, as Snowflake doggedly plowed under another low-hanging branch, she cursed the fact that she'd insisted she didn't want his gallantry.

"Snowflake, darn you," she groused under her breath. "I thought you were supposed to be docile. Don't you know what *docile* means? It means you aren't supposed to try to kill me every five minutes!"

Looking up, she realized she was once again separated from the others. Unfortunately, they'd entered the deepest part of the woods, and the trees were as thick as quills on a porcupine. She glanced around and sighed. "Thanks, you bag of ornery bones. Do you see any of the other horses?"

She could hear the kids laughing and shouting. But from what direction? Frowning, she tried to determine where the sounds were coming from. It seemed like they were off to her right. She kneed her untrusty steed, and shook the reins. Snowflake angled left. "No—no!" Jess complained. "Are you doing this on purpose? Go right! Right!"

Snowflake whinnied, arched her neck saucily and lurched to the left, lurching directly under a branch so low that Jess couldn't crouch down enough to escape. In desperation, she slid from the saddle and landed in a heap on the ground, her foot still tangled in a stirrup. Groaning, she yanked it free. "Fine. My backside's already hamburger, and now you hurl me down on the part of my anatomy that's sorest, you—you escapee from a dog food factory!"

Snowflake who had smelled water, snorted and plodded toward the stream close by, to get a drink.

Jess gave the departing mare a murderous scowl and rubbed her painful hip. As she stood up stiffly, she thought she saw a glint of something white. She squinted and peered more closely. It looked like a white wooden wall with a green shutter. A cottage in the middle of nowhere? "Hmm," she mused. "Hansel and Gretel's place? Or, with my luck, it'll belong to the wicked witch." She started after Snowflake, who was drinking noisily in the nearby stream, but remembered that she and the horse weren't on speaking terms. She left Snowflake, her nose down in the swirling water, and wandered off alone.

The little cottage wasn't far away through the trees. It was surrounded by a white picket fence; the gate was locked. Inside the neatly trimmed yard, an ancient oak tree mushroomed high above the wood-shingled rooftop, and an old-fashioned tire swing hung from one of its sturdy lower branches.

There were big old azalea bushes on either side of the small, covered porch that held a weathered rocker. Gingham curtains hung prettily in the windows. Jess could imagine the windows open, the curtains fluttering in the breeze. The little white cottage nestled picture perfect in the forest seemed untouched and pure. Jess had the feeling that she'd stepped back in time into someone's gentle childhood. Who in the world lived here so simply and charmingly?

The fence was only waist-high, so she managed to climb over it without much trouble. First, she knocked at the door, but when there was no answer, her curiosity got the better of her, and she went around the side to peek in a window.

"Why, it's lovely," she murmured aloud. The cottage had only one room with a rough-hewn wooden floor, which was scattered with colorful rag rugs. A smoke-darkened stone hearth divided the far wall in half. On the far right was a wood-frame bed covered with an old hand-stitched quilt. On the left side of the room, rustic kitchen counter and shelves lined the wall. There was nothing on the counters—no sign of a sugar bowl or a bread box, no signs of recent occupancy.

Between the kitchen and bedroom areas, near the hearth, was a couch covered by a blue-and-white-striped horse blanket. Opposite it sat a couple of easy chairs that had seen better days. Separating the chairs from the couch was a round pine coffee table, and on it, a china teapot on a tray. Though the place was as clean as a pin and free of dust, it had a sorrowful, un-lived-in look about it.

Jess scanned the hearth more closely. There were no ashes, and no firewood was stacked, ready to light. Several partially burned candles were grouped at one end. On the opposite end of the stone mantel sat several framed pictures. Jess strained to see, but couldn't quite make them out.

"They arrest people for what you're doing," came a stern voice. Jess jumped and turned to face a very tall, very grim-faced Lucas Brand. He was sitting astride his black stallion, just beyond the fence. "You scared the hell out of me when I found your horse back there— riderless. I thought you'd been thrown."

She grimaced. "I *was* thrown— Well," she amended sheepishly, "maybe it was more . . . scraped off, like the burned part on toast." She rubbed her hip again. "That darned brute hates me."

Lucas's expression eased slightly. "Want a lift?" He held out his hand.

Eyeing him dubiously, she said with a weary sigh, "I don't know. I've fallen off enough horses for one day, I think."

He dismounted and stepped easily across the white picket barrier. "Come on. I'll make sure you don't fall."

She was reluctant. The specter of failure loomed again, and her stomach pitched despondently. "Maybe I'd better just go get Snowflake and glue myself in the saddle."

"Have you always been such a rotten horsewoman?" he asked, lounging against the fence.

She hugged herself, rubbing her arms partly in nervousness, partly because the late afternoon was bringing with it a chill that was seeping through her bulky wool sweater. "I guess it depends on the horse," she murmured self-consciously. "This one isn't a very good sport."

"I don't blame her. Poor girl."

"Poor girl!" she scoffed. "More like wild-eyed assassin! She knocked me off on purpose!"

"She picked up a rock somewhere. Didn't you notice her limping? Probably seemed cantankerous because your weight was causing her pain." He coaxed with a small nod. "Come on. You can apologize to Snowflake while we take her back to the stable."

Jess wasn't happy about this plan. But she supposed she'd better ride. She had no idea which way Lucas's house was, and the sun was setting rapidly. Stifling a sigh, she said, "Okay, but don't expect me and that horse to kiss and make up."

They went back over the fence at the same time, Lucas making quicker work of it, with his much longer legs.

"Would it offend you if I helped you up?" he asked.

She turned to stare at him, feeling awkward. "I can get up by myself," she muttered.

He nodded his assent, but there was skepticism in his expression that told her very plainly, I won't interfere with your Don't-do-anything-for-me-or-it'll-prove-I'm-a-failure requirement, but I think it's nuts.

Jess lifted a foot into his stirrup, grabbed the saddle horn, and swung a leg up and over. Once settled, she eyed him with proud hauteur.

Their glances clashed and held. After a moment, he said, "Too bad nobody but me was here to see that mounting triumph."

She was taken aback by his sardonic remark, and even more stunned when he joined her in the saddle and his body surrounded hers in a most intimate way. She grew flustered. "There's not much room—is—is there . . . ?"

With his hands about her waist, he shifted her onto his thighs. "Better?"

She was grateful he couldn't see her face, which had gone cranberry red, she was sure. Clearing her throat, she rasped, "It's— I'm fine. . . ."

Taking the reins, he began to guide them back to where Snowflake and her bruised foot waited. Jess turned to look at the cabin once more as they rode away. Aloud, she wondered, "Who lives there, Lucas?"

He said nothing, just held her butted up against him, clenched between arms that expertly held the stallion's reins. His scent invaded without warning in the chilly, early-evening air, filling her with an unruly desire to lean against his hard strength. Even more strongly, she felt a need to turn her head and meet his lips, which were bare inches from hers. Knowing no good could come of such a crazy act, she held herself stiffly away, resisting with every fiber of her being.

It took her a full minute of worrying about her rapid heartbeat, wondering if he could feel it—or even worse, hear it—to realize he'd never answered her question. "Lucas," she began again in a whispery tone. "That house is on your property, isn't it?"

"Yes," he said, without further explanation.

"Well?" she prompted. "Who lives there?"

"That's none of your business, Jess," he warned softly. "Drop it."

She was confused and irritated, not so much by his refusal to answer her, though that made her curious to know more, but because his breath was warm against her cheek. And his sturdy chest, bumping her every so often, was so inviting. His scent, which she was breathing now with every intake of air, was like an aphrodisiac. She recalled his kiss again in all its startling perfection, and closed her eyes, thrilling at the memory. Her mind began to float away in a sepia haze filled with sexy scents and passionate kisses, and she found herself losing the fight to resist.

No longer concerned that she was a weak fool, she gave in to her need, and tilted back against him, a tiny, still-functioning part of her brain praying she wouldn't regret this lapse. But something else in her, an unexpected urgency, drove her as she relived, in her mind, how utterly sinfully the man kissed.

He was so disturbing, she shivered, dreaded, yet yearned to share something—everything—with this man....

As soon as she relaxed against him, she sensed a reticence in the sudden tensing of his body. But seconds later he shifted forward, his tongue caressing her ear. "What's happening here?" he murmured.

She turned into his amorous overture and groaned, "Nothing..."

"Good," he whispered, dipping his tongue provocatively, sending tingles of delight through her body. "Because we shouldn't get involved."

"I know." She shifted closer, wanting to taste his lips again, driven by her willful craving. "I—know. We shouldn't..."

He leaned forward, gathered her in his arms and held her snugly as he reclaimed her lips with a force that was blinding and beautiful. She moaned at the contact, struck again by the power of his kiss. It took away her will, making her his to do with as he pleased.

She clutched at his thighs, then hugged his arms even more tightly to her, frustrated that he was at her back. She wanted to press herself to him, wrap her legs around his hips, know the feeling of his erection as he entered her, making her writhe with the fulfillment she instinctively knew he could give. If his kiss was this staggering, leaving her lips burning, what must his lovemaking be like? Never had she felt such an exhilarating reaction to any man's kiss. Intuition told her that Lucas Brand was her perfect mate—at least sexually. And that message was hard to ignore as his lips, teeth and tongue both thrilled and tormented her in his dizzying exploration.

Needing to be closer to him, she slid a leg up, hooking it around the saddle horn, and instinctively leaned farther back into his arms. He responded by crushing her to him, his demanding mouth plundering hers, his tongue working magic. And Jess, her body humming with want, gave back everything with a savage intensity she had never experienced in herself. It was as though she'd awakened from a long night into the electrifying stimulation of a spring storm. She was alive, her senses quickening with sudden new appetites. She was a woman, and she found herself glorying in that fact for the first time in her life.

Lucas gritted out an oath and muttered against her lips, "I want you so badly I could take you right here in the woods. Is that what you want?"

She clung to him, her eyes tightly closed, as though that would keep out the consequences of right and wrong. She didn't dare answer, for the sound of her voice might break the spell. She only wanted to stay here, to be held in his arms, know the bold heat of his mouth and his body forever. Without words, she slid one wayward hand down to caress the bulging juncture between his legs. She felt giddy and light-headed.

She sighed against his mouth. "Oh, Lucas—" She broke off, embarrassed to voice her longing, but her hand massaged, and learned the sort of information a woman shouldn't know about a man she was better off not making love to. She knew he was ready for her, fully capable of satisfying her, right now. And from the fondling she'd recklessly initiated, she knew she would rather die than go away without experiencing the full extent of Lucas's sexual prowess.

He groaned, and moved a big hand down between her legs to match her movements. She grew limp from the sensual excitement he caused. He held her tightly to him, and Jess could feel the quiver of his muscles through his sweater from the tension of supporting her weight, and of holding himself back. "Jess," he whispered roughly, "do you want it in the woods, on your back in the leaves?" He paused, kissed her hard, taking her breath away as his fingers massaged, sending jolts of pleasure along her limbs. "I'm not sure it's fair to you, but hell, we both know we'd be good together. It's your call."

She couldn't believe it, but his stroking, even through her jeans, was rushing her toward climax—on the back of a horse in the woods. She clasped him to her, crying out in lusty little gasps, "Oh—oh—Lucas—don't stop...." With trembling fingers, she stroked his denim-sheathed erection, delighting in the dangerous intimacy as she spiraled over the brink, quaking, whimpering softly in disbelief.

She just lay in his arms for a long, lovely minute. Weak and tingling with afterglow, she lifted her arms about him, burying her face in his chest. She relished the hammering of his heartbeat and the sexy heat from his body. She'd never met a man who was so hazardous to her moral standards, but ironically, she was far from upset by her lapse. She wanted to remain here—within his wildly exhilarating embrace—forever.

"What are you thinking?" he murmured after a long pause.

She snuggled closer and sighed helplessly. "That's never happened before."

"What?" He held her slightly from him. "You've never come with a man before?"

Her face grew fiery as she shook her head. "No—I mean, not with my—my clothes on."

She could feel a small chuckle rumble through his chest. "Or on the back of a horse, I'd guess."

She looked up into his face and smiled timorously. "Or on the back of a horse."

He was watching her with a masculine hunger that unnerved her. Still, he said nothing, made no move to kiss her again. It was her decision to make. Did she want him to make love to her, or didn't she? She saw the heated question in his eyes.

Yes! she wanted to cry out. *Yes, Lucas! I long to know the feel of your hands on my body, the touch of your devastating lips tasting private, secret places....* She swallowed again, feeling herself dampen at the mere idea. But she knew her fantasy was far from wise. Lucas wasn't the kind of man who could ever settle down and be content with a wife and children; he was too driven by power and success.

She'd been through all that with Porter, and she'd have to be the worst kind of fool to let it happen again. With one last look into those dark, questioning eyes, she reluctantly pushed away, uncurled her leg from around the saddle horn and turned her back on him. "I—I'm sorry," she whispered. "I know you'll think I'm the world's worst tease, but you're right. We shouldn't get involved." Reaching forward, she picked up the discarded reins and held them out to him.

He understood her cue, and kneed his horse forward. When they neared Snowflake, he captured the mare's dangling reins and muttered huskily, "Come on girl. Let's us cripples go back home."

JESS LAY IN HER BED, staring up at the ceiling. She'd spent a long, hard evening, watching Lucas from under low-

ered lashes as he went about his Mr. Niceguy duties,
making hamburger patties, helping set the table and,
after dinner, mopping up the kitchen. It was fascinat-
ing seeing him do his part. She supposed he'd simply
decided to get it done as quickly as possible. Then he
could get up to his darned computer room to spend half
the night working on his business problem.

Rolling over on her side, she wondered how he continued to function, being with the kids all day and
working at his computer all night. She recalled his face
this evening after dinner when he'd chanced to glance
her way. His eyes had been shadowed with fatigue, but
the look he'd aimed at her had been anything but weary.
His scorching gaze had traveled up and down her, then
clashed with hers for a long moment, flashing a sexual
communiqué that made her melt with yearning. She'd
been immobilized by the message there. It frustrated her
almost to the point of screaming to know with such
certainty that she and Lucas would be explosive in each
other's arms, but that they dared not risk the compli-
cation. Then, unexpectedly, he'd simply turned away,
leaving her feeling utterly desolate.

Recalling his look now, she shivered. That look had
been erotic, full of sexual promise, disturbing—even
across the distance of the room. Their extreme physical awareness of each other had only intensified since
this afternoon, and even now, in her lonely bed, she
could feel it thrumming relentlessly through her veins
and plaguing her mind, destroying her rest.

She checked the bedside clock. Three twenty-three.
She'd been dwelling on this subject so long she was at
her wit's end. She had to get Lucas Brand out of her
mind. He was definitely not a man she wanted. Too

much like her father and her husband. Self-assured and aggressive, with little time or patience for a family. And Jess desperately wanted kids, and a man who would sit by a cozy fire, reading to his children, laughing with them, wanting to share their lives. She didn't see Lucas Brand in that picture. But that didn't keep her heart from craving him in her bed.

Almost mad with exhaustion and need, she bolted up, and with a defeated groan, slid her legs over the side. This was the most lunatic thing she'd ever done — or would ever do—but tonight, she planned to get this obsession with Lucas Brand finished, once and for all.

LUCAS RUBBED HIS EYES as the computer screen blurred before him. He checked his watch. Three-thirty. With an weary grimace, he kneaded his temples, then went back to work. Tried, anyway. His thoughts had been haunted by Jess all night. Her fragrance lingered in his nostrils, harassing him. Good *God*, he'd never wanted a woman as badly as he wanted her. He fisted his hands, wanting to rip out trees by the roots, or toss cars off cliffs. He needed to dispel this raging sexual energy she'd provoked in him, and then left so frustratingly unfulfilled.

He couldn't blame her, but that didn't keep him from wanting to yank houses from their foundations. He and Jess were obviously extremely compatible sexually. It was just too bad that their wants and needs—other than sex—were so incompatible.

"Welcome to horny-bastard hell, Brand," he muttered bitterly to himself.

"Lucas?" came a distant, but familiar voice. He twisted around to see Jess standing inside his closed office door. He was surprised that she'd come in without his noticing.

She was wearing a knee-length terry robe and her feet were bare. He frowned in confusion.

"Lucas?" she repeated, moving closer. He detected the light scent of her perfume as she asked, "May I talk to you for a minute?"

He nodded, still perplexed. Maybe working day and night for weeks brought on hallucinations. He hoped he wasn't that far gone, and tried to shake off the absurd idea.

Her expression was somber, and her eyes held that familiar, lurking nervousness. But there was more lurking there, an odd determination. He wondered what bee she might have in her bonnet now.

As she stood before him, she began to loosen the tie of her robe, keeping her eyes pinned on his. With a small shrug, she let the garment fall to the floor. Lucas's heart stopped, but other parts of his body came to full, bursting life when he saw the slim loveliness of her body.

Before he could speak, she opened her hand, displaying two condom packets. "I—" she began, then faltered.

Amazed but delighted, he stood, taking her into his arms. "Are you sure about this?"

She molded herself to him, as though it had taken all her strength to get here, and she had none left. Leaning into him, she looked up into his eyes, her expression distraught. "I have to do this," she whispered plaintively. "I'm sorry, but I have to get you out of my system."

He frowned down at her. "And you think having sex with me will do that?"

She bit her lower lip, her eyes glistening. "I hope so, Lucas."

He felt a surge of irritation, but couldn't be angry with her as she clung to him, soft, willing and naked. With a wry half-grin, he grazed a kiss along her cheek, grousing, "One day that truthfulness of yours is going to kill me."

"I—I'm sorry, but—" Her voice broke. "I can't go on having useless fantasies about someone I don't want in my life."

He felt a rush of tenderness and regret so intense it was painful. "There's a lot of that going around," he said, knowing he'd lost too much sleep for the same damned reason.

"When you—do it, don't try very hard," she pleaded faintly. "I—I don't want to like it. I just want it over...."

He could feel her tremble in his embrace. *Holy hell.* Jess Glen might be a failure in the eyes of her parents and her ex-husband, but to him, she was a woman with an iron-willed honesty that beat the devil out of anything he'd experienced in his life. Her impetuous candor was unique and touching in a world of oily smiles and white-collar bull.

He wanted to hold on to that for a while, wanted to make love to her like he'd never loved any other woman. Wanted her to touch him, hold him and smile at him with the same warmth he'd seen in her smiles at the kids.

The bottom line was, he couldn't give her the emotional commitment she needed. He'd trained himself to dominate his emotions, avoid involvements. But getting to know Jess had become a unique and troubling experience.

Sure, he'd had women come to him, wanting a quick fling. But Jess's plaintive request wasn't the same thing at all. Little Miss Heart-On-Her-Sleeve didn't want a night of fun. She needed a sexual-reality check that would restore her peace of mind. And if he was honest with himself, so did he. Everybody knew the fantasy was always sweeter than the reality. It was better to find out, get it over with, and move on. But, somehow, holding Jess like this dulled the harsh edge of his self-imposed isolation in a way no other woman ever had. It was an unsettling realization.

Where was his famous, cool-headed logic? Usually a naked woman in his arms was not a problem. He simply made love to her and forgot her. So why was he hesitating? Possibly because he had a nagging suspicion that if he took her up on her offer, there'd be an emotional price tag when it was over—one that might be very, very steep.

"Lucas?" she asked, searching his face. "What is it?"

He could see raw vulnerability in her eyes, and knew she feared he was going to reject her. And to her that would be a thoroughly humiliating failure to add to what must be, for her, a lifelong list. He muffled an obscenity in her sweet-smelling hair. He didn't want to hurt her, but he was far from sure that having sex with her was the wisest route for either of them.

Against his better judgment, his fingers roamed downward, along the silky contours of her back, to cup a tempting hip. He groaned, going hot and rigid with desire. Abruptly, deciding not to think or analyze, he lifted her into his arms. *"Dammit,* Jess," he whispered gruffly. "You never make anything easy."

Wrapping her arms about his neck, she offered sadly, "I'm sorry—"

"Quit saying that!" he growled. Looking around the sparsely furnished room, he mused aloud, "There's no comfortable place in here to make love."

"That's good," she whispered, bleakly. "Uncomfortable is good."

He bit off another curse. "If you want uncomfortable, how's the floor?"

She nodded. "Probably as uncomfortable as any place."

He shook his head at her and lowered her where they stood. "At least let me spread out this robe."

She removed her arms from about him and watched as he opened her bathrobe on the polished wood floor. His mood grim, he glanced up at her. *"Hell.* Don't look so much like you're being burned at the stake."

She lowered her gaze to her clenched hands. "Maybe you should start getting undressed."

"Why don't I just unzip my pants?" he suggested sarcastically. "That'd be more slam-bam-thank-you-ma'am. No real involvement."

She swallowed visibly. "If you prefer."

He glowered at her. "Well, I *don't* prefer. I'm not going to treat you like a ten-dollar trick, no matter how quickly you want me out of your system. Is that clear?"

She blinked, and lifted her unhappy gaze, but said nothing.

He was torn. This was the craziest situation he'd ever been in. "Look," he began more gently, leaning toward her and grazing her lips with a kiss. "You brought two condoms. If you want it over so fast, what was the second one for? Tossing a water balloon on the gardener's head? He gets here in an hour."

She flushed all the way to the pink tips of her breasts, and he felt a hot tightening in his gut at the sight. "Either we do this for real, or we don't do it at all." He hated saying those words. If she grabbed up her robe now, and left him kneeling on the floor, he doubted that he'd ever walk upright again. But some things couldn't be compromised or rushed, and he had a strong conviction that making love to Jess Glen was likely to be one of them.

Her glance fluttered away for what seemed like an eternity, then returned, more direct and determined than ever. "I—I suppose, if those are your terms, I'll have to agree." She lifted her chin, the image of Joan of Arc on the brink of martyrdom.

Relieved that she was still there, he smiled ruefully. "If it'll make you feel better, I'm probably lousy in bed. And on a hardwood floor, it's practically a given."

"I'm counting on it," she mumbled. "Kiss me, Lucas."

Experiencing a bizarre mix of frustration and elation, he lowered her gently onto her back.

10

JESS SCARCELY FELT THE hard floor or the terry at her back. Her whole being was focused on the face above hers. His chiseled features were serious, yet striking. She felt completely defenseless against this man's charisma. No longer able to fight it, she ached for his touch.

As he made a move to get the lights, she grabbed his hand. "No, don't," she implored. "No romantic lighting. I want to see all your flaws." Her eyes welled in her frantic need to know Lucas Brand as nothing more than the self-centered being she was sure he was—not the sensitive lover her crazy intuition was trying to convince her he could be.

A shadow of annoyance crossed his face. "No bed, no soft lights," he muttered. "How many stipulations are you going to put on this thing? Maybe we shouldn't even kiss."

She lay there, very aware that he had placed an arm intimately on either side of her breasts, his shirtsleeves grazing her nakedness. His body warmth was inviting, and his scent, so masculine, turned her on, making her damp with want. Unable to help herself, she reached up to stroke his jaw. "I couldn't bear it if you didn't kiss me, Lucas." Her lower lip trembled as she scanned his disapproving face. "I wish I could be strong and say no kissing, but I can't—not with you."

The frustration in his eyes faded, and with a rueful twitch of his lips, he shook his head. "Dammit, Jess." He turned into her hand, kissing her palm. "Dammit . . ."

He lowered himself gradually, and as he did, she slid her arms about his neck, drawing him ever nearer. The act seemed to be played out in slow motion, every second an eternity of anticipation. At first, his lips only brushed hers, and she found herself straining upward for more.

Running her hands through his hair, she smiled into those hypnotic eyes. "Come here," she invited, surprised at the seductive purr in her voice.

His mouth met hers, coaxing, pleasing, and she was nourished with the utter sweetness of it. She curled her arms more tightly about his neck and drew him over her to blanket her body, instinctively spreading her legs. He groaned and moved against her, so that she could feel the bulge of his erection at the moist juncture of her thighs.

He showered hot kisses along her jaw and throat, working deliciously downward, his lips fiery, driving her mad.

He slid off and drew a hand along her side, inch by inch, making her body tingle. His fingers tempted her ribs, her hip, her thigh, then traced across to her pulsating core, where they dipped, making her gasp and arch with the lightning flash of gratification his touch elicited.

As his fingers stroked and penetrated, she found herself panting and gasping for air, breathless with the wild rush of feelings as he probed deeper, more insistently, teaching her things she didn't know nice well-brought-up girls did. But with him, everything was so natural, so wonderful and right.

He fondled and fanned into flame the most secluded reaches of her sexual core, eventually making her cry out in climax, quaking, her body glowing with exertion.

When her breathing had calmed somewhat, he drew her into his embrace, and she snuggled against him, savoring the denouement of her climax, thrumming pleasantly through her body.

A big, gentle hand cupped her hip, another stroked her hair. His breath was intoxicating as it whispered along her face and shoulder. She was aware of the strength and heat of his hard body, still sheathed in all his clothes. "Why," she breathed weakly, "do you keep pleasing me, and never yourself?"

His low chuckle tickled her breasts. Kissing the tip of her nose, he asked, "Do you think watching your orgasm bores me?"

She felt her whole body flush, and buried her face in his button-down chest. "Oh, Lord," she groaned, trying to shut out the vision of herself losing control before him. Mortified, she recalled the lewd words she'd uttered in the mindless moments when he was driving her wild, masterfully guiding her into exhilarating fulfillment. "I'll never be able to look you in the eye again," she cried. "I said some filthy things."

He drew her more tightly to him, and she could feel the steady beat of his heart. "You made some sexy requests," he teased, his hand on her hip stroking provocatively. "If you meant them, I'll be glad to oblige."

She shifted to look into his eyes, then lifted her hands to his shirtfront and began to unbutton it. "I'm afraid I did," she whispered, kissing the parts of chest that were becoming exposed to her view.

His hands stroked and massaged as she unbuttoned his shirt. Stunned with the rapidity at which this man could make her crazy with desire, she cried out, and unthinkingly, ripped the shirt open. Buttons flew and bounced about them in a fitful rat-a-tat on the floor. "Oh—" Jess breathed, unable to keep from hugging him, flesh to flesh at last. "I—I'm sorry for ruining your—"

His fingers plunged and she cried out with stark, delirious ecstasy.

"*Never* apologize to me again," he commanded huskily in her ear, his tongue matching the movement of his fingers, driving her over the edge of another lightning-intense climax.

After she helped him remove the rest of his clothes, they lay naked in each other's arms for a moment. Jess's body was slick and tingling from having been so utterly pleasured by a man she'd mistakenly thought cold-blooded and mechanical. She'd never been so mistaken in her life. Sexually, Lucas was proving to be a wild man, a sorcerer shrewd in the ways of satisfying and indulging a woman.

He knew how to tantalize to the edge of insanity, for he had not yet attempted to enter her. He just lay there, his hands roving seductively, his lips making hot little demands along her shoulder blade. Languorously, she scanned his lean, muscular body. It was flawless—unfortunately—even in the stark light of the room. Unable to stop herself, she took hold of him and stroked his erection with awe and reeling anticipation. "You're killing me," she cried. "This much restraint can't be good for you—you'll have a heart attack."

He grinned down at her, his expression full of sexy promise as his hand slid across her belly to fondle her breasts. "I feel fine," he said, his voice low and amused. "But, thanks for your concern."

Jess closed her eyes, sure that at any moment she was going to die from sensory overload. She moaned, writhing helplessly beneath his touch as currents of new, primitive hunger washed through her. Clutching at his broad torso, she feared she was going to explode if he didn't enter her quickly. In a broken whimper, she pleaded, "Lucas, please— Love me . . . *now* . . . ."

His body shifted to cover hers, blocking the light, and the room grew dark. He touched her intimately, probing, tantalizing her as he positioned himself. The sensation was thrillingly erotic. He hovered for a spellbinding moment, and she licked her lips expectantly.

His thrust, when it came, was a lovely shock. Urgently, potently, yet lovingly, he entered her, and she gasped at the sweet torture, her whole being filling up with him.

At first his movements were slow and measured, while he gradually drew her toward fulfillment. Then, becoming more and more aroused, she wrapped her legs about his rock-hard thighs, and pulled him deeply into her, welcoming him, making love with a ravenous passion she'd never before experienced. As he began to plunge more forcefully, new hunger spiraled and blazed in her, and she delighted in his unexpected recklessness.

The sounds of their lovemaking were sounds that Jess knew she would hear echoing in her dreams for the rest of her life. Their love was beautiful and uncivilized. Untamed, unwise—and evanescent. Realizing this, she felt a sadness invade her pleasure.

Almost desperately, her hands searched, held and worshiped the exposed, lean muscles of his buttocks and back. She moaned his name again and again as the extraordinary power of his surging body consumed her totally. She was swept away on wave after wave of sensation, both alien and exquisite, until at last, molten shafts of rapture exploded inside her, and she cried out, abandoning herself to the cresting climax.

With a ragged groan, he shuddered inside her, holding her possessively to him as he found his own release. Their lips met in a stormy kiss of mutual triumph. And, trembling, Jess clung to his broad back, utterly fulfilled, utterly consumed.

When their lingering kiss ended, she lay still there for a long moment, her mind dazed, her body like jelly. Joined to him, and redolent with his scent, his delicious nakedness still pressing her to the floor, she felt as though she were in a dreamworld—a world from which she had no desire to wake. She sighed, and kissed his shiny-wet flesh, and she ran a hand along his spine, delicately, dreamily.

"What are you telling me?" he crooned near her ear. "You want more?"

She opened her eyes at the sound of his voice, drawn reluctantly back to reality. Her tone sorrowful, she sighed, "Oh, Lucas . . ." She uncurled her legs from around his muscular thighs. "I don't have the stamina for more."

He smoothed a damp tendril of hair from her temple, replacing it with a kiss. "What about the other condom?"

Her eyes widened. "The *condom?* I completely forgot. And this is—is a bad time of the month for me to be careless."

His gaze was caressing. "It's okay. I remembered."

"But," she stammered. "When? I never—"

He grinned at her. "Your mind was somewhere else at the time."

She flushed hot. "I have to admit my mind has never deserted me as totally as it did tonight." Swallowing hard, she whispered, "You must think I'm very loose."

He frowned, then flashed a provocative grin. "I thought nothing of the kind."

She became uneasy under his gentle scrutiny. It occurred to her that he really did have plans for using that other condom tonight. Long, strong fingers were already trailing down her rib cage, making her tingle with renewed sexual excitement. She couldn't let it happen. This insanity had to stop before it was too late—before she fell in love. She squelched a mental voice that was trying to tell her something—something she dared not hear. "Lucas," she began thickly, brushing away his hand. "I—I didn't mean for us to get involved. I just wanted..." Her voice broke, and she found that all she could do was turn her head away in a wordless plea to be released from the heavenly male confines of his body.

He said nothing for a time, but his hand no longer quested along her skin. Finally he lifted himself away from her, gently disconnecting them. But Jess flinched at the parting, sure she had experienced something almost mystical with this man, yet, knowing him the way she did, determined she must never yearn for more. He had no place in his heart for a wife or kids. Fantasies and dreams of a future with him were useless.

"Am I out of your system?" he asked, sounding solemn.

She tried to shut out the harsh truth, loath to admit it even to herself—that she would *never* forget this man; *never* be able to put this night out of her mind. Because of her foolish weakness for him, she would be cursed to relive what had happened here for the rest of her days—*and nights.*

Fearing her voice would betray her, she only nodded, trying to coax her weakened limbs to move. Before she could escape, he wound a hand roughly through her hair and drew her lips to his, scorching them in one last, taunting kiss. She sagged against him as his mouth sapped her of the desire to do anything but draw his hot, powerful erection into her again.

As she was about to wrap her arms about his broad shoulders and drag him back down to blanket her—to put to lovely use that remaining condom—he whispered huskily against her lips, "Let me get this straight. Your bottom line is, you found out what you wanted to know. Now we move on?"

She pulled back and studied his face. He was regarding her with dark, earnest eyes.

She looked away unhappily, then struggled to her feet. "That's about it."

Lucas scooped up his slacks and stood, also. "I see," he said. "There's just one thing."

Jess had plucked up her robe and was searching for the armhole, but his ominous tone stilled her movement. "What?" she asked.

"Some people might say that's a little cold-blooded," he softly rebuked.

His quiet censure unstrung her, and she countered defensively, "Oh? Well, why don't we ask Mary Anne Brown her opinion of *you?*"

His eyes flashed with anger, but a tentative knock at the door shattered any further debate. Horrified at the thought that someone might find her in such a compromising position, Jess fumbled nervously and dropped her robe.

He frowned, snatched up her robe and tossed it at her as he called out, "Who is it?"

"Maxim, sir," came the hushed reply.

"What is it, Maxim?" Lucas asked. He struggled into his slacks as he motioned for Jess to get behind the door. When he'd thrown on his shirt, he pulled the door open. Jess cowered, not daring to breathe. "What could be so important at this time of night?" he asked, sounding more weary than angry.

"Sir," Maxim began, then paused, coughing as though embarrassed, and began again, "I'm sorry to disturb you, but there was a call on the house phone for Mrs. Glen, and..." He paused again. "She doesn't seem to be in her room."

"Thank you, Maxim," Lucas said. "I'll handle it."

When the door was closed, Jess finished putting on her robe, whispering fearfully, "Do you think he suspected?"

Lucas's expression turned cynical. "I don't know. Maybe he thinks I caught my shirt on the computer keyboard."

Jess scanned the dress shirt he'd tossed on. One lone button dangled from it. She cringed to think how he must have looked to his butler—with his torn shirt, its tail out, and his belt undone. She had to admit he didn't look much like a man who had been quietly occupied working on a computer program! "Oh, *Lord*," she moaned. "He knows. He must have heard us!"

"Maxim doesn't gossip," Lucas assured her tersely as he headed to his desk. Pressing a button, he lifted the receiver. "This is Lucas Brand. May I help you?"

In the waiting silence, Jess cinched her robe belt tightly and padded over to the desk. She watched Lucas's expression change from angry to perplexed. "Yes, I understand. I'll tell her." He hung up.

"What is it? Didn't they want to talk to me?" she asked, worry coiling along her spine.

He turned to face her, his expression troubled. "Get dressed," he said, an unspoken question clouding his eyes. "That was the police. It seems they have your mother in custody."

THOUGH JESS HAD INSISTED that Lucas absolutely *not* take her, he refused to wake Jerry, and was emphatic about driving. His Ferrari was too small, so he grabbed up keys for a BMW sedan and practically shoved her inside while she protested vigorously. How humiliating for him to see her mother, Mamie Ritter, having one of her attacks of premature senility, claiming she was Mamie Eisenhower, first lady of the land. Now, huddled in the car with her mother who was going on and on about some imaginary dinner party, she watched Lucas's profile as he headed away from the precinct station.

"Straighten your shoulders, Jessica," Mamie scolded. "How many times have I told you? And what sort of costume is that? Jeans? After all your father and I've said about such plebeian attire? Gracious sakes, the president's daughter should remember her image." She sighed theatrically. "Mr. Brand, do explain to Jessica about first impressions. A man of your stature in the community. Perhaps she would listen to you."

Jess chewed the inside of her cheek and stared out the windshield. Heaven only knew what Lucas was thinking. She shuddered, hugging herself in dismay. Now, not only had Lucas made love to her and dismissed her as cold-blooded, but he'd had to bail her mother out of jail! Porter had *left* her because of Mamie's looniness. Being a greedily class-conscious man, he'd slammed out of the house one day, shouting he couldn't have business associates over with Mamie liable to go loony tunes at any time.

"Those silly policemen," Mamie chattered on. "How dare they treat me with such ill regard." Though she was sitting farthest away from Lucas, she reached across her daughter and patted his thigh. "You're a prince to come to my rescue, dear. Do you recall our meeting when you bought my husband's firm? Or did we meet?" She tapped her chin in thought. "Well, no matter. Jessica," she reiterated, without pause, "what are you doing, sunk down there like a spineless rag doll." She reached over and pushed her daughter's bangs back. "And get that scraggly mess off your pretty face. What if a reporter snapped you that way? Would you want to look all slumped over and hairy like a beatnik on the front page of the *Daily News?*"

"Mother, please," Jess begged tiredly. "We'll be home in a minute. You need to get some rest."

"Oh..." Mamie complained, suddenly sounding like a frightened child. "Don't make me go back there, Jessica. It's so—so lonely. I get scared."

Disconcerted, Jess ran both hands through her hair. Mamie had been doing pretty well for the past month. Apparently this separation had preyed on her mother's nerves, making her regress. "It'll only be five more days," she promised faintly.

Mamie burst into sobs, and covering her face, wailed, "You're so mean to leave me. I'm your mother, and you just desert me this way!"

Jess had to put a fist against her lips to keep them from trembling. Taking a deep breath, she worked at regaining her composure.

Before she could speak, Lucas startled her by asking, "Isn't there somewhere she can go?"

Dejected and at a loss, Jess blurted unhappily, "You mean *besides* the White House?"

For a few minutes, Mamie's sniveling was the only sound in the tense quiet. Jess searched frantically for a solution to the problem with her mother. She didn't want to have to put her in some sort of home. Mamie would hate that. But her mother was becoming a problem when she got off on these Madam President tangents. "Mother—what about your knitting, or needlepoint? I thought you were enjoying—"

"Oh, you *hate* me. You're an ungrateful girl, and you want to forget me—*bury* me before my time," she bawled.

Jess cast a glance toward Lucas to gauge his degree of disgust at her mother's histrionics. His profile was rigid, and she could see a muscle working in his jaw. Her battered heart fell to her toes. First she'd practically bulldozed him into having sex with her, which accomplished nothing but to ensure his eternal contempt, and now he was being forced to witness her private hell—a tantrum from her befuddled, spoiled, and domineering mother. Jess really didn't blame him for his hostility. To make matters worse, she'd acted like a shrew. With a sigh, she shook her head and looked down at her hands, fisted in her lap.

"Mrs. Ritter," Lucas said, in a deep, curt voice. "First, I regret that we never met." Mamie looked over at him, still sniffling, as he went on, "Secondly, I'm sure you're aware of who you are, and you pulled this stunt because you were lonely and wanted attention. Am I right?"

Mamie screwed up her face at him. "That's very impudent talk, young man."

Jess watched her mother haughtily fluffing her stylish silver hair. She didn't know if she should rebuke Lucas for speaking harshly to her, or if he might not have a point.

"I'll make you a deal," he went on. "You behave, and you may stay at my home for the next five days. With your daughter."

Jess gaped at him, openmouthed.

"Why, Lucas, dear," Mamie exclaimed, pulling a handkerchief from her bag and blowing her nose. "That's a lovely invitation. I'd be charmed." Flourishing the hankie, she turned to Jess and fairly preened. "You see, Jessica. I *told* you Mr. Brand wasn't the ter-

rible man you said he was. Just because Clancy left me
for that teenage trollop after he sold Lucas the company, and because Porter left you when I came to live
with you, doesn't mean Lucas Brand was *completely* to
blame." She reached across Jessica to pat Lucas's thigh
again, assuring grandly, "I forgive you, dear, and I'm
sure Jessica will, in time. I always knew deep down you
were a gentleman. Breeding always tells!" She sighed,
and clasped her hands to her breasts. "I've heard your
house is simply exquisite. I can't wait to see it for myself."

Jess blocked out the rest of her mother's ramblings,
and shrinking lower in her seat, she squeezed her eyes
shut. Now Lucas knew everything there was to know
about her—the irrational hatred she'd harbored for him
for the past five years, and the sad truth about her
mother's deteriorating mind. But most distressing of all
were the things he'd heard her say tonight—the erotic
things she'd cried out as he'd brought her to climax after exhilarating climax. Her stomach clenched at the
white-hot memory, and she wished she were dead. Why
must there be *five* days of this dratted retreat left—five
horrible, humiliating, endless days? And now her
mother would be there to make them even more humiliating and horrible—and endless!

Jess settled Mamie in the room opposite hers, then
caught Lucas in the hallway. Her emotions had run the
gamut tonight. She was exhausted and upset, and she
had the worst headache of her life. Her anger with herself for her stupid attraction to Lucas gnawed at her.
And to add insult to injury, she was having to deal with
the nagging shame over her mother's condition.

What she *really* wanted to do was to fall into his arms and have him hold her, tell her everything would be all right. She wanted him to be gentle and concerned. Her whole body quivered with the desire to have him kiss her soundly and tell her he cared, and that she would never have to feel like a lonely failure again. She wanted to hold him to her and tearfully thank him for being so sensitive about her mother. Unfortunately, their hot sex on the computer-room floor came back to haunt her, and she knew any rekindling of that earlier scene would be foolhardy.

She wiped the corner of her eye with the back of her hand to hide a sudden welling of tears. "Look," she hissed, urgently, "I—I appreciate what you did, but I don't want your pity and neither does my mother."

The tensing of his jaw betrayed his sudden umbrage. After a taut silence, his lips twisted cynically. "Baby, I don't think you know *what* the hell you want. You hate me, but you have sex with me?" His chuckle was bitter and angry. "I wonder if there's a Hallmark card for that—maybe, 'Hi there, I hate your guts but I'm horny, so drop trou—!'"

Jess flinched at the ferocity of his words, though they had been spoken barely above a whisper. "Lucas, it's true," she tried weakly. "I did hate you, but since we've gotten to know each other, I—"

His laughter sharp and brittle, he cut her off. "*Know* each other?" he echoed incredulously. "That's quaint." With a lightning-swift move, he swept a provocative finger between her legs, growling, "Yes, I'd say we'd gotten to 'know' each other, baby." Turning abruptly away, he stalked off toward the stairs.

Jess sagged against the wall, her body resonating with the hot, tingling sensations he'd so calculatingly set pounding in her core. She balled her fists, her nails biting painfully into the flesh of her palms, feeling thoroughly shamed.

11

THE MORNING CREPT BY with the speed of a turtle on its back. Representatives from the University of Oklahoma and Oklahoma State gave presentations about career opportunities. The kids were attentive, and best of all, Lucas was gone.

Since Jess hadn't had any sleep, most of her morning had been spent struggling to keep from falling off her chair in a heap. She imagined Lucas must be having the same problem at his office. Today was Careers and Crafts Day, so he'd been granted time off.

She was managing to keep awake with lots of coffee, but the Goodalls and the Kornblums were giving her odd looks. She didn't blame them. Every time they smiled at her, she yawned back.

"Madam?" Maxim inquired, startling her from her fuzzy ramblings. She leaped a foot off the chair and gasped. All the kids twisted around to rubberneck. Howie Goodall stopped in the middle of his talk about the joys of leather craft, and stared in confusion.

She bit her lip, mumbling, "Excuse me. Please—go on, Howie." She hated having to face the butler, who knew what a sinful night she'd spent with the master of the house. Unable to look him in the eye, she whispered, "Yes? What is it?" half expecting a blackmail demand.

"Mr. Lucas is on the phone."

Her heart hammered stupidly against her rib cage at the mere mention of his name, and she glanced at Maxim's sober face. "He wants to talk to—to me?" she breathed faintly.

"It seems your mother is at his office."

"Mother?" Jess felt a stab of apprehension "I thought she was sleeping...." As she rushed toward the kitchen, she called back, "Thank you, Maxim," and meant it in more ways than one. The servant's eyes had been gentle, almost pitying, in fact, and she was grateful. "What's happened, Lucas?" she said breathlessly as she picked up the receive. "How did—"

"Your mother's fine," he interrupted. "She was doing her Mamie Eisenhower impersonation, and the police were going to throw her in the drunk tank. To make a long story short, she convinced a patrolman to bring her here."

"There? Why, there?" Jess asked, confused.

"I don't know," he said tiredly. "But I haven't ruled out industrial sabotage."

"I'm coming right down." She hung up and found Jerry tinkering in the garage. Twenty minutes later, she rushed into Lucas's high-rise office where a group of men, their ties loosened and jackets discarded, were huddled in fierce discussion. Behind their circle of chairs loomed some spaceship-like computer equipment, much the same as that installed in the room at Lucas's house where they so recently—

The men glanced her way en masse, and an expectant hush fell over the room. She imagined they were waiting for her to explain why she had suddenly turned a bright shade of pink. Some movement caught her attention, and she noticed a plumpish woman wearing a classic blue suit, her short silver hair immaculate, her smile hostess-bright.

"Mother...?" Jess breathed.

The woman lifted her gaze from the cup she was filling. "Why, Jessica," came the huffy response. "Can't you see we're in the middle of a meeting? Shame on you for interrupting. We haven't much time to work out a problem with our horse-feedbag glove. Do we, dear?" She directed an extravagant smile at Lucas.

Nodding perfunctorily, he strode to confront Jess by the door. "She might as well stay," he said under his breath. "All she wants is to keep busy and feel important. I'll bring her home with me."

Jess's anxious glance swung from him to her mother, who was offering to make sandwiches. With a worried sigh, she looked back at Lucas. "I'm—I'm sorry—"

"Quit apologizing for things that aren't your fault," he broke in sharply. "We're busy. Just go."

"You look awful," she said, without thinking. The skin beneath his eyes was deeply shadowed, his craggy features drawn in exhaustion. She had a foolish urge to hold him, to try to put the gleam back into his dark eyes—the gleam she'd seen for a brief moment last night when they were lying in each other's arms. Squelching the memory, she scolded, "You need sleep."

His tired yet mesmerizing gaze searched her face. "You should have thought of that last night," he admonished softly.

With a hot, liquid rush of feeling, she veered away from that dangerous subject. "Lucas, is any amount of money worth ruining your health?"

"*Dammit*, Jess. I'm not the only one to consider here," he gritted. "There are stockholders—"

"Oh, sure, and they'll go bankrupt without this deal?"

"No, but Takahashi's contract would be our biggest this year. Our stock value would go up at least—"

"I'm all aquiver," she scoffed. "Think what a nice big tombstone you'll be able to afford!"

She watched his brow crease into a scowl, but before he could speak, Sol called, "Brand, come see what you think of this idea."

He nodded absently, growling under his breath, "Look, I know you can't help being a bleeding heart. But I'm busy. Go bleed on somebody else."

"Okay. *Act* like a hard-nose," she hissed. "But, you called me about my mother and kept her out of jail, busy or not."

He'd turned away, but stopped to flick her a puzzled glance. "Anybody would have done that. What's your point?"

"My point is, you try so hard to be a hardass," she insisted. "But a *real*, hardass wouldn't have cared enough to call, and certainly wouldn't allow her to stay and—"

"Lucas?" Mamie interrupted, with a wave. "Do you want chicken salad on wheat or ham on rye? I'm doing both."

He held up a finger to indicate he'd be right there. "Stay the hell out of my *head*, Jess," he warned, wheeling away to rejoin his meeting.

On the trip back to the house in the limousine, Jess couldn't banish the surge of affection for Lucas that had come over her in his office. Heaven only knew, she'd tried. Not only had he *not* been embarrassed by her mother, but he'd given her a "job." Even as harried and exhausted as he was.

Darn you, Lucas Brand, she complained inwardly. *The last thing I want in this world is to harbor tender thoughts about you! Why aren't you the cold-blooded jerk you pretend to be?*

BUT HARBOR TENDER thoughts she did, even though, for the next two days, Lucas kept his distance. She'd felt a completely illogical disappointment about that.

Tonight was the hayride, and Lucas and Jess were chaperons on the second wagon. She knew the less time she spent with him the better it would be for her mental health in the long run. But she kept dwelling on the fact that he'd have to be near her for several hours, and her heart thrilled. Unfortunately, Mamie had decided to ride along, so Jess tried not to get her hopes too high.

Surprisingly enough, after Mamie's sojourn in Lucas's office, she'd begun to behave better. She'd taken over as a sort of "warden of etiquette" at mealtimes. To the amusement of the volunteers, Mamie gave spirited lectures on table manners, utensil placement and the proper rendering of thank-you notes. Even though she became confused sometimes as to which meal was which, she was more an asset than a hindrance, and the kids seemed to find her a strange but interesting addition.

Mamie dressed like a proper president's wife, and continued to harangue Jess about her "vulgar" choice of clothing. But oddly enough, the kids appeared to feel better about themselves at the very idea that they, one day, might have to write a thank-you note to the governor for a "lovely time." It was true that one former Oklahoma governor and a current United States congressman, were products of the Mr. Niceguy program. So, who really knew what might happen one day? If nothing else, it wouldn't kill the teens to be able to write a proper thank-you note or identify a shrimp fork.

Seven o'clock rolled around, and Jess was emotionally torn about sharing anything so intimate as a ten-foot-long hay wagon with Lucas—rolling along under a pale gold lovers' moon. Would he talk to her? Maybe even smile?

Soon enough, she discovered she needn't have worried. Mamie had made it her duty to station Lucas at the front and Jess at the back, while she took a post in the middle. That way, her mother explained, they could all keep a sharper eye on any "potentially immoral" activities that might get started beneath the blankets.

Jess and Lucas didn't speak two words to each other, or share so much as a glance, all the way to the site of the bonfire and weenie roast. Around nine, the scent of burned weenies redolent in the air, Jess realized her mother was missing. "Oh, no," she moaned, glancing frantically around. Mamie had insisted on wearing a three-piece tweed suit and low-heeled pumps—her idea of casual clothing. If she got lost in the woods, she'd freeze before morning.

Catching Bertha Kornblum by a coat sleeve, she whispered, "Mother's disappeared. I'm going to look around. She gets disoriented so quickly."

Bertha nodded. "Don't go far. Even with the moon, the woods are pretty black."

Nodding, Jess caught a glimpse of Lucas. He was at the makeshift condiment table—a blanket spread over the back of a hay wagon—smiling and talking with Jack and Annie. Though Lucas looked tired, he appeared to be relaxed and was clearly enjoying himself. While Jess watched, the dog, Moron, scampered up, and stole a weenie out of Jack's bun. Jess heard Lucas's deep laughter and felt strangely desolate. All she craved was a simple smile from the man. Why, she wondered, must she care? Remembering she needed to locate her mother, she headed into the woods. "Mother?" she called softly, not wanting to alert the others until it became absolutely necessary. "Mother? Where are you?"

Jess reached a stream, and was amazed to recognize the spot. It was near that quaint white cottage. She peered around. Yes, there was the darned branch that had scraped her off Snowflake the other day. Instinctively, she headed for the natural bridge formed by a fallen tree that spanned the creek.

"Mother?" she called again, stepping onto the trunk. "For heaven's sake, this is no time to go wandering off." A voice inside her suggested that maybe she should heed her own advice, but she didn't have time to ponder the wisdom of it. Something ahead of her moved. She squinted and recognized it as an animal of some kind—with a long, white— "Oh, my Lord," she breathed. *A skunk.*

She pivoted on the log to backtrack, and was horrified to see another skunk on the far end of the log, with several smaller ones trailing behind. Had she stumbled into some sort of skunk parade? A polecat family on an outing?

The absurd circumstance that had put her in the middle of a log bridge between a touchy-looking mother skunk and her offspring on one end, and perhaps, dear old Dad on the other, wasn't important right now. What was important was—she was *trapped!*

She ran through her list of options quickly. It was short—get squirted by an irate skunk, or get wet. Taking a deep breath, she slipped into the stream, clamping her jaws to stifle a cry at the icy chill of the water.

Remaining as still as she could, she stood statuelike, afraid to breathe, as the mother and her offspring crept across the log at eye level.

Once they'd disappeared into the blackness, she sucked in a long-overdue breath and hugged herself to ward off the violent tremors that flooded her body.

"Let me guess," came a deep, amused voice. "You're going down with the ship?"

Lucas stood on the bank, his lanky legs braced wide, his arms folded across his chest, a crooked grin on those firm, sensual lips. He exuded that maddening sexual magnetism she knew so well, and had fought so hard. She stared longingly at him, thinking maybe a dip in the freezing water was worth seeing him smile again. A violent shiver brought her back to her situation, and she retorted through chattering teeth, "I love f-funny men. Why don't you g-go look for one!"

"You're catching your death." He leaned forward, extending a hand. "Grab hold."

Since the other bank was steep, she had no choice but to move toward him, but she ignored his offer. "N-no thanks." Even his casual helping hand would be hard to bear, now that she knew what those hands could do....

He cursed, grasping her by the upper arm and hauling her out. "At the rate you're moving, you'll freeze solid," he said, hoisting her into his arms. "You'll have to get out of those things."

"I can't g-go back." she objected weakly. "Mother's lost."

"No, she's not. She was out—'using the facilities'— to put it in her delicate terms."

Jess relaxed as much as her quivering muscles would allow. "Thank heaven." Looking around, she discovered they weren't headed toward the campfire, but were crossing the log bridge. "Wh-where are we going?" she asked, her teeth making loud, clacking noises.

"The cottage." He sounded reluctant, as though he had no desire to take her there. "You can get out of those wet things."

Just as Lucas stepped off the log and onto the bank, there was the sound of barking, and Moron rushed past and disappeared into the woods. "Damn dog's going to be pleasant company on the trip back," Lucas mused with a resigned shake of his head.

She eyed him speculatively. "You saw the skunks, then?"

He met her gaze. "Yes."

"And you didn't try to help me?"

"I left my tranquillizer gun at the office," he drawled, a faint smile quirking his lips. "Anything I'd have done would have set them off."

She realized he was probably right and dropped the indignant tone. "Moron'll get lost," she murmured. "We're pretty far from the house."

"I doubt it," Lucas said with a mordant chuckle. "The worse he smells, the faster he finds the house. It's one of Murphy's newer laws." They reached the clearing and he stepped across the picket fence.

"You don't sound particularly unhappy about it," she commented softly. "You've changed, Lucas."

He set her on the cottage porch and reaching up over the door, fished for a key. "I'm just too tired to care," he muttered, as he inserted it in the lock. The scarred portal creaked as it swung open. Lucas stepped back to allow her to precede him. "Take off those wet things. I'll get a fire going."

He crossed the room to the hearth, opened a rough chest, and lifted some cut wood from it. He'd placed several logs in the hearth before turning to peer at her. She was still shrinking near the door. "Get those things off," he repeated more sternly.

She swallowed hard. "Don't you think it's a little inappropriate? I mean, you being right here and all."

A dark brow lifted sardonically. "I've seen you naked," he reminded harshly. "You made sure of it. Remember?"

She floundered before the intensity of his look. "I— Well *that* was—"

"I know what it was," he cut in, and went back to readying the fire. "And since we're past having any sexual interest in each other, you should have no problem shedding wet clothes in front of me."

She hesitated. "Of—of course," she answered feebly, and scurried across the room. She wrapped the quilt from the bed around her and skinned out of her sopping clothes. Lucas didn't turn in her direction as he added pieces of kindling to the fire, gradually coaxing it into a healthy blaze.

She perched on the bed, pulling her legs up to hug her knees beneath the quilt. Unable to help herself, she watched his profile. His thick black hair, lit by the flickering firelight, gleamed a rich mahogany. His square jaw was tense, and something like pain was etched into the grave lines of his face.

She felt suddenly restless, and got up. Remembering her discarded clothes, she swept the quilt about her, taking the clammy things to the fireplace to drape them from the stone mantel. The two photographs sitting there drew her attention, and she picked them up to move them into a better light.

Settling on the rag rug before the glowing hearth, she peered at the silver-framed images. One was an elderly woman, kindly looking, dressed in overalls and a man's plaid shirt, her gray hair twisted into a bun atop her head. She looked careworn but lively, and there was something familiar about her eyes. The other photograph was of a small boy standing between a scroungy mutt and a swaybacked horse. The child was dark-headed, and had the most wonderful smile....

Her mouth dropped open in mute surprise. "Why, Lucas." Holding up the boy's picture, she said, "This is you, isn't it?"

He'd stopped stoking the fire, and was just sitting there beside her, watching, apparently dreading the question. A muscle worked in his jaw, as he nodded. "In another life."

She frowned at his sad response, holding out the photo of the woman. "Who's this?"

Clearly impatient, he grabbed the pictures and stood to replace them. "I'll go tell your mother to gather some dry clothes when the hayride's over. Then I'll—" He dragged a hand through his hair. There was frustration in his gruff voice—the same frustration that had settled in the depths of his eyes. Unexpectedly, he turned away and strode toward the door. "Somebody will bring you your clothes and get you home." Before she could object or even register that he was leaving her there, alone, he was gone. The only sound was the echo of the slamming door.

Jess tried to rest as she waited, but couldn't. She wandered restlessly about the cottage, haunted by the memory of Lucas's troubled face. She was forced to finally admit to herself that she cared about Lucas. Since it was clear he didn't plan to tell her about his past, she felt compelled to search through the cabin's meager contents. She desperately needed to know everything she could about him.

As she rummaged in drawers and cabinets, she carried with her the two framed pictures. She didn't find much. Dishes, pots and pans, an old metal jewel box with a few trinkets inside. The thing that drew her interest in the box was a folded, hand-drawn Valentine inscribed with the childishly scrawled message, "I love you, Grandma Jane." The signature had read, simply, "Lucas."

There was also a faded snapshot of a man and woman. The man bore a striking resemblance to Lucas. Jess guessed that these were his parents, in happier times, before addiction to drugs had ruined their lives.

From these skimpy keepsakes, she gleaned a great deal about how Lucas had become the man he was. It seemed he'd lost everyone he'd ever loved, one way or another. As a small child, he must have felt utterly abandoned, first by his parents' desertion, then by his grandmother's death.

He'd mentioned he'd been married once. Jess had a feeling his marriage had come at a time when he was beginning to heal, to reach out. When it ended, he'd simply closed himself off entirely. A tear trailed down her cheek. She brushed it away, closed the box and replaced it in the dresser beside the bed.

So, this was the reason Lucas Brand tried so not to care for people. He feared abandonment so much, he'd shut himself off from emotional connections. He made sure he discarded relationships before they could discard him. That's why the Mary Anne Browns of the world waited in vain for his call. He'd promised himself never to put his heart in jeopardy again. She couldn't really blame him. People defended themselves from hurt in many different ways. Lucas had obviously chosen to place his trust and his passions in the logical, unemotional world of computers.

And this cottage had become a shrine of sorts, a cherished monument to what he'd called "another life"—a life in which he'd felt loved and secure, one that his young, broken heart had convinced him could never be his again.

A footstep on the porch made her stiffen. Then she realized it was someone returning with her clothes. When the door opened, she stared in astonishment and her breath caught in her chest. Lucas stood there.

Framed in the doorway, an overnight bag clenched in his hand, he was painfully arresting, clad in close-fitting jeans and a bulky white turtleneck that accentuated the width of his shoulders. Firelight and shadow played on his solemn face, giving it a bold and primitive look. Silently, he entered the cottage and closed the door behind him.

She held herself very still, the familiar heat of desire washing over her against her will. "Lucas," she breathed. "I thought— What are you doing here?"

He dropped the bag on a chair, quickly closed the distance between them and crushed her in the strong warmth of his arms. "Damn me to hell if I know why," he growled, his tone hoarse with self-reproach. "I may be out of *your* system, Jess. But, you're not out of *mine*." Lifting her, he settled her on the bed, then hovered inches above her, imprisoning her between his arms and the looming promise of his body. "Give me tonight," he coaxed roughly, his eyes searching hers with such erotic purpose that her heart turned over in response.

Her thoughts in a jumble, she swept her gaze over his face, down his lean cheeks to the sharp, chiseled lines of his tensed jaw, then back to his lips—those wonderful, tormenting lips that could thrill her to mindless distraction. There was nothing she wanted more in life than to give herself to him—now and all the rest of her days. But having discovered his fear, his reason for rejecting love, she was terrified to let herself say yes. She didn't want to be just another Mary Anne Brown to him. She loved him. She knew it now, and that knowledge filled her with trembling dread.

"Lucas . . ." she tried, but her voice failed her. Frantically, she turned away, struggling to maintain a shred of composure. "You have a right, I suppose, since I—I started this thing." He didn't answer, forcing her to look into his blazing eyes.

"Don't talk like a failure. You don't owe me a thing," he ground out. "Don't give yourself to me as a sleazy consolation prize. You're an intelligent, accomplished woman, Jess. Either you want me, or you don't." His dark, compelling eyes raked her face, searching for truth. "Just *tell* me what you want. It's as simple as that."

Oh, if it were only that simple, Lucas! her mind cried. But her foolish willful arms paid no heed as they curled about his neck and drew him down to her.

12

HIS KISSES WERE blissfully bruising and she gave herself freely to his passions, knowing that what they shared tonight would have to last her for the rest of her life. Tomorrow was the final day of the retreat. After the barn dance and closing ceremony, the kids and volunteers would vacate Lucas Brand's grounds—and his life.

It was hard to imagine that only a scant two weeks ago she'd despised this man, thinking him cold, like her father and her husband. But now she knew that beneath the aloof facade he was a feeling human being, a truly nice guy—but a man afraid to be vulnerable.

Jess had only a few short hours to indulge in the joys of his hidden, passionate side. The tender hunger of his kisses shattered her, a heady punishment for her foolishness in beginning this crazy affair. But she couldn't feel any regret while his tongue was sending shivers of desire through her, and the hot exploration of his hands made her body tremble, and her limbs cling to him desperately.

His lips trailed down, deliciously teasing, and she moaned in anticipation. With each tormenting kiss, he paused to whisper risqué plans for every inch of her body, and she grew weak with need. Big hands captured her hips and his mouth found its destination between her thighs. His deep kiss sent her reeling, and she cried out, squeezing him to her with trembling legs, squirming under his ministrations, her breathing coming in high-pitched gasps.

His touch was inspired, its raw sensuality carrying her to ever-greater heights, until at last, she careened wildly over the edge into a soul-stirring climax. She writhed and quivered, unable to control her cries of pleasure.

While the afterglow seeped through her veins, a deep sense of peace entered her. She sighed languorously, and caressed the thick hair at his temples. "Come up here, Lucas," she demanded, her voice throaty and breathless. "I want to feel you inside me."

His wily tongue gave her one last, bawdy tribute. She arched up, her blood surging with the thrill of renewed arousal. When he slid forward to cover her body with his, she held him tightly, kissing the crook of his neck, his jaw, his lean cheek, until at last their lips met, his descending on hers with ravenous longing.

The kiss sent delicious sensations flowing like warm honey throughout her body. They clung to each other, their mouths communicating a profound, wordless message. The encounter was extraordinary, suffused with something almost sacred, beautifully sensual, yet reverent. It was as though their souls had become mystically blended, and now were joined—forever.

Lucas must have felt it, too. Suddenly, he lifted slightly away, and stared into her face, a flash of uncertainty in his eyes. His features grew dark and troubled.

"What is it?" she asked, her voice frail and love-thickened. "You look like you've seen a ghost."

A bleakness washed across his features, and his eyes glistened. "God, Jess . . . I . . ." He broke off, swallowing hard.

"Lucas?" she asked, fearful.

In a voice rough with desire, he muttered, "*Damn,* I'm sorry," and slid off, leaving her feeling bereft. He stood, wiping a shaky hand through his hair. "Get dressed," he commanded gruffly. "I'll wait outside."

Her body ached desperately for the fulfillment he'd withdrawn. She pleaded, "Lucas, what did I do . . . ?"

"*Nothing,*" he barked, scowling. "Forget it. Forget *me.*" Spinning around, he stomped off. "Get dressed," he demanded, again, his tone dismal.

Jess was surprised she was able to push herself up, she felt so unsteady and helpless. The world tilted around her, and she wasn't sure if she was awake or if this was some dreadful nightmare she couldn't manage to shake off. "Lucas, *why?*" she cried, covering her face with her trembling hands.

She heard the door close and realized Lucas hadn't heard her grief-stricken entreaty. But did it really matter? Deep down inside, she knew the answer. She'd sensed it in his kiss, seen it in his tormented face. Lucas had felt affection for her tonight—possibly even love— and he hadn't been able to cope with it.

She knew now how utterly useless it was to harbor hopes for a life with him. He'd chosen to exist in a cold meticulous world that had no place for emotional attachments or imperfection. She had no recourse, no argument. She huddled on the bed, shivering, her body still moist and tingling from his loving, wishing she could go back to believing him cold and heartless.

Aching with sorrow, she understood him now, understood his demons, and knew she loved him, in spite of the fact that he would never allow himself to love her. A heartbroken sob escaped her throat. Surely she must be the world's biggest fool!

THE RETREAT ENDED ON a decidedly sour note. The last of the activities, a barn dance, went off without a hitch, but Jess's head ached so badly she could hardly be civil. Needless to say, Lucas's riveting presence didn't help much. Yet, somehow, they both made it through the evening with pasted-on smiles. She gave her Work Hard and Succeed speech, and Lucas made a few unexpectedly charming goodbye remarks.

Amid the final hugs and parting tears, Lucas surreptitiously passed Moses a package. Jess was confused at first, then realized he hadn't forgotten his Mr. Prick promise, and had given the boy some condoms. She was surprised he'd remembered, and the act touched her.

She was surprised again, minutes later, when several of the teens gave him small parting gifts they'd made while on the retreat. Jess watched, saddened. The kids had grown quite fond of their substitute Mr. Niceguy. Unfortunately—so had she.

His face clouded at being singled out for tribute, and Jess sensed he was feeling more embarrassment than he displayed. He accepted the offerings in a low detached voice. Considering his philosophy of noninvolvement, he would certainly back away from any growing fondness for the kids, just as he'd backed away from his feelings for her. Indignantly, she wondered how long it would be before the humble, heartfelt tokens ended up in Lucas's trash.

She glimpsed him as he headed from the barn toward the house. He'd said nothing to her. No goodbye. No smile. Not even a scornful nod of good riddance. He'd simply walked off and disappeared into the darkness.

A rectangle of golden light appeared in the distance—the broad, black silhouette of Lucas's familiar torso, signaling the fact that he was entering his mansion. As the door closed, extinguishing the glow framed within it, Howie started the van. More depressed than she'd ever been in her life, Jess sank low in her seat, rubbing her pounding temples. She winced as the vehicle lurched forward.

"MR. BRAND," LUCAS'S secretary called loudly near his ear.

Surprised that he hadn't heard her before she'd had to resort to shouting, he swiveled around from his discussion with Sol and Fletch. "What is it, Debbie?" he asked. "If it's Takahashi again, tell him we can make the meeting in Tokyo on Friday."

"Yeah," piped in Fletch, a big smile on his weary, freckled face. "*Finally* the glove responds, and we're one-hundred-percent on track. With only Mega-Tech left in the running, I can almost smell that contract."

Sol, who'd been wearing the head-mounted display and working the glove, took the equipment off, started to stand, stuttered something, then slid off the chair onto the carpet.

Lucas, Debbie and Fletch stopped their conversation and stared at the chubby man, crumpled in a heap at their feet. "He looks a little flushed," Fletch said, more to himself than anyone.

"Hell, he looks *dead*," Lucas muttered, stooping to check his friend's pulse. "Sol, what is it?" The fallen man blinked as Lucas felt his face. "Damn, you're burning up."

"I'll call an ambulance," Debbie cried, rushing from the room.

"Could be that new flu," Fletch put in. "Sol's been working pretty hard. Probably let his resistance get low."

Lucas frowned. "I'm surprised we're not all dead. Let's get him over to the couch." He raised Sol up so his friend could lean heavily against him. "Can you walk, or do you want me to carry you?"

Sol groaned, stumbling. "I'm fine—just a little tired...."

"Blast it, man," Lucas ground out as he and Fletch half dragged Sol to the couch situated behind the computer equipment. "People who've been hit by trains look healthier than you."

As Sol collapsed on the sofa, Debbie hurried back in, looking more upset than Lucas had ever seen her. "Ambulance is on the way," she reported, her expression stark with concern. "And—Mr. Brand, there was another call for you, a young lady—Miss Ann Smith—"

"I don't know any Ann Smith," he interrupted, preoccupied with his friend's condition.

Debbie nodded, turned to leave, then stopped and added, "It's only that she asked for Mr. Niceguy, sir. But I'll tell her you're busy."

Lucas had knelt beside Sol to find out if he was breathing regularly. But something Debbie had said nagged at his brain. Ann Smith? Mr. Niceguy? "Annie?" he intoned, thinking aloud.

JESS PEEKED INTO THE children's hospital ward. It had been four days since the retreat ended, and she'd never expected that the next time she saw the kids, they'd be crowded around a hospital bed, and sweet, shy Molly Roberts would be lying in it with a broken leg. Molly's bed was the one nearest the door in the ten-bed ward. Only four beds were occupied. Jess was glad Molly had friends around her, considering that her foster-home situation was far from ideal. It appeared the kids from the retreat had bonded into an extended family.

"Hi, Mrs. Glen," Annie called in a loud whisper. "Join the party."

Jack was there, a bit apart, as usual, but not quite frowning. "Hi, everybody." She checked her watch. Four-thirty. "What did you all do, come here right after school?"

Moses said, "No sweat. Bus stops in front. But man, this place freaks me out. Too many sickos."

Jess laughed, turning to Molly. In the hospital bed, with her cast raised up in a pulley contraption, the young girl appeared thinner, more fragile. "Annie told me you took a header down the school steps," she said with a sympathetic smile.

Molly's big, gentle eyes looked sheepish. "It was dumb. I dropped my glasses and—" she shrugged "—I was trying to grab them before they broke and didn't watch where I was going. But the school was great, and they're paying for all this—" she swept a thin arm about "—and they're fixing my glasses."

"That's fine." Jess felt a sad tug at her heart and came over to perch on the bed. She noticed the cast held the kid's autographs. "May I sign?" she asked, indicating the marking pen sitting on the bedside table.

"Oh, sure." Molly smiled cheerfully.

A large bouquet of flowers also sat on the table beside the bed. Jess had noticed them when she first came in—a big bouquet of miniature pink rosebuds and tiny cream-colored carnations amid a delicate cloud of baby's breath. The arrangement was perfect for a young girl like Molly. One expected to see flowers in a hospital room, of course. This arrangement, Jess realized, must have cost at least fifty dollars. Far out of the range of Molly's friends.

She touched a diminutive rose. "Where did these come from?

"Mr. Niceguy," Molly whispered. "He brought them himself."

"Oh, that's lov—" Jess halted, her eyes widening in confusion. "Mr. *Who?*"

Molly was looking at the bouquet now, her plain features animated with happiness. She reached for an envelope and handed it to Jess. "Look at this."

Jess fished out ten small pieces of cardboard, then realized they were tickets. She scanned them, reading aloud, "'Whitney Houston Concert. December fifteenth. Oklahoma City Pavilion.'" Her words died away as she looked up at Molly. "These are impossible to get. And they're right down front," she murmured, more to herself than anyone. "Where did these come from?"

"Mr. Niceguy brought them," she repeated softly. "He told me to make sure everybody from the retreat got one." She relaxed back against her pillows with a dreamy expression. "I'm going to get better really fast, now. Whitney Houston is so cool."

"She's thick, man," Moses added with a leer.

Jess glanced at him, feeling woozy from the mere possibility that Lucas Brand had not only managed to get tickets—which must have cost him a fortune from some scalper—but he'd delivered them *himself*. And flowers, too? She scanned Moses's face, trying to keep her mind on track. "Thick? I presume that no longer means stupid?"

Moses chortled. "You pre-*zoom* straight."

"It means she has a good body," Annie explained, sounding irritated. She gave Moses a sharp crack in the ribs with her elbow. "You are *so* annoying, jerk-face." She said it with a flirtatious smile, and everybody laughed.

There was a throat-clearing from the door, and Jess turned to see Jerry, Lucas's chauffeur. "Say, Jack, dude!" he called with a grin. "Gotta go."

Jack, who had been sitting quietly behind the main group, stood and nodded at Molly. "Check you later," he offered, with the beginnings of a surprisingly charming smile.

Molly smiled back and blushed. "Give Moron a hug for me."

Spitball, who'd been eating what looked like left-over pudding from Molly's lunch, set the empty bowl aside and kidded, "If that mutt stinks like usual, he'll have to give him a tomato juice shower first. Peee-uuuu!"

"Hi there, Ms. Glen," Jerry said with a wave when he noticed her.

She smiled and waved back, feeling confused. Once Jack and Jerry were gone, she asked, "Where are they going?"

"Oh," Annie said, "Mr. Niceguy hired Jack to come out and do chores, and take care of Moron—like clean him up when he comes home stinking. Jack goes out there every day after school, does his homework and a few other things around the place, eats dinner, then Jerry takes him home." She leaned back in her straight chair and glanced furtively at Moses. "See, Jack wants to keep Moron, but the apartment building where he lives won't allow pets, so Mr. Niceguy's letting him sorta keep Moron this way. That Mr. Niceguy is totally awesome." She added proudly, "I'm the one who called him and told him about Molly being in the hospital, and we talked about a bunch of stuff."

Jess stared. "You did?"

"Yeah. First time, he had to call me back, but he's major cool." She gave Moses a coquettish look and added mischievously, "And a total *stud*."

Moses snorted and rolled his eyes, and Jess detected the touch of jealousy she was sure Annie had been hoping for.

After that, she lost track of the conversation. The image of Lucas as a "total stud" was too upsetting, considering their fiery sexual past. She tried to think about other things—like the things Lucas had been doing for the kids. Was this the same man she'd met just two weeks ago? It hardly seemed so. Unable to control her unhappiness, her soul cried out to him, knowing even as she did, that it was hopeless. But why, oh, why, couldn't his softening extend to his feelings for her?

She supposed she knew the answer. A few tickets, flowers and an after-school job were a far cry from committing to marriage and a family. Lucas had obviously come a long way in two weeks, but he would never allow himself to fill the emptiness in her heart with a vow of love.

Over the past four days, she hadn't for one minute been able to put Lucas's face from her mind—especially as it was that last time she'd seen him, with that haunted expression when he'd left her at his cottage. Why did she have to love a man who couldn't allow himself to care for people? Overwhelmed by a sense of desolation, she swallowed back a sob.

"Mrs. Glen?" Spitball asked loudly, obviously trying to get her attention. "What?" she squeaked, then cleared her throat. "Yes, Spitball?"

He indicated the pudding bowl. "You think they have any more of that brown stuff? It's funky."

Moses grunted. "Hey, man, you come here to see Molly or starve her skinny butt to death?"

They all laughed and jostled Spitball, who reddened and grinned sheepishly. Jess struggled to concentrate on the kids' jabbering about what was happening in school and their excitement over the upcoming Whitney Houston concert. She tried to put the elusive Lucas Brand from her mind, and failed, dismally.

LUCAS SAT IN THE BACK of his limo on the way to the airport, going over some last minute notes. His corporate jet was leaving for Tokyo in thirty minutes. He hadn't expected to make the trip alone, but Sol was still in the hospital, recovering from flu and exhaustion, and Fletch was on a second honeymoon at the insistence of his wife, who'd hysterically demanded either he go away with her for two solid weeks or *she* was gone!

Lucas hadn't minded giving Fletch the time off. They all needed a rest. Besides, he didn't relish ruining a friend's marriage. He'd ruined his own—at least that's what his wife had said.

Long ago he'd purposely cast off all involvements. He'd never wanted to deal with the pain of loss again. The last time he'd gotten emotionally involved was when he'd married Karen. She was nineteen and he was twenty. They were both in college, and were happy for a year—until Lucas discovered she was into hard drugs. He'd thought he was doing the right thing when he'd intervened and had taken her, kicking and screaming to get treatment. He'd cared, *dammit*. He'd loved her, and had done everything in his power to help.

Having seen what drugs had done to his parents, he'd tried to save his young wife from the same fate. But, had she thanked him? No. Instead of running into his arms after she'd gotten out of the hospital, she'd divorced him. He'd been devastated, had tried to talk to her for two years, but no. She'd have none of it. None of him. Then, three years later, he'd heard she'd died of an overdose.

Lucas tried to refocus on his work, but as he'd found so many times over the past six days, it was impossible. Jess's face kept appearing before him. *Damn her. Damn her lovely, animated eyes. Damn her honest, sympathetic heart, her entangling personality.* Her effect on him was undeniable. He admitted that. But aside from wanting her, aching for the silken feel of her body, the taste of her lips, moist and hungry against his, had he ever done anything so stupid as fall for her?

"Dammit, no!" he muttered with angry emphasis. More forcefully than necessary he pressed a switch that opened the window between his chauffeur and the large passenger area. "Jerry," he barked. "We could make better time if you avoid the construction coming up on—" He halted midsentence, his chauffeur's squawking police scanner catching his attention. "Did they just say a *Mamie* Ritter had been missing for over thirty-six hours?"

"Huh?" Jerry asked, angling the stretch limo into heavy traffic. "What, sir? I—"

"Quiet!" Lucas sat forward, and strained to listen. The dispatcher was relaying that a woman in her fifties by the name of Mamie Ritter, of Jess's mother's description, had been missing since yesterday morning.

Lucas scanned the cityscape with apprehension. Snow was coming down hard, driven by an icy wind, making visibility poor, and the forecast called for five to six inches before nightfall.

He could see Jess now. Distraught, but trying to be brave. "Hell," he growled between clenched teeth. He had to be in Tokyo tonight. The multi-million-dollar deal rested on his shoulders. Stockholders were depending on him. The board of directors was foaming at the mouth, making dire threats if he didn't get this contract. There was no way Fletch could be reached, no one who could go to Tokyo in his place. Besides, he told himself sternly, Mamie Ritter was *not* his concern.

The rationalization tasted bitter in his throat. He hadn't realized until this moment what a powerful hold Jess had on his feelings. He was suddenly contemplating tossing away everything he'd worked so hard for, to look for a demented woman who was probably renting a room at the best hotel in town registered as Mamie Eisenhower. She was most likely just fine. The intelligent plan would be to go back to his notes, fly to Tokyo, make his presentation, and continue being the successful, solitary millionaire he'd worked so hard to become.

He exhaled a low oath. Ever since that instant in the cabin with Jess, when he'd realized . . . Well, he'd panicked and run. He hadn't stopped running for nearly a week since he'd last seen her, and he was still running. Soon he would be half a world away.

He was furious with himself for allowing his emotions to manipulate him like this—to even give a thought to Jess and her problems. He'd believed he was beyond caring and the pain it could cause, and he was angry to discover he wasn't. Why had Norman tossed

Jess Glen into his well-oiled life so she could throw it out of kilter? "Damn woman," he grumbled, and leaned forward to ask Jerry, "What kind of time are we making?"

"Fine, sir. Snow's not too bad, yet. We'll get to the airport with no problem."

Lucas could hear the dejection in his driver's voice. Jerry liked Mamie, and it was clear he wasn't pleased by the idea of the poor woman out wandering aimlessly in subfreezing weather.

The afternoon light was dying, with the sun buried alive behind the swirling early-December snow. Lucas gave his watch a harried glance, feeling vacant and spent. Fatigue seeped from every pore. He'd be able to sleep on the plane, he thought. It was damn overdue.

The elegant limo slithered through the snow and downtown traffic, toward the highway that would take Lucas to the airport and away from any risk of involvement with Jess Glen or her troubles. *Good riddance*, he swore, mentally.

He scanned the buildings as they rushed by. Concrete and glass, drab and inhospitable, even when softened by the veil of eddying snowflakes. Never before had he seen his high-rise world with that jaundiced eye. Maybe what Jess had said out there in the woods was true. Maybe, he *had* changed. One thing he knew: The excitement had gone out of his work. He frowned, at the notion. His work was his life, his passion. *Nothing has changed*, he told himself sharply. Running a distracted hand through his hair, he slouched back in his seat and called out, "Jerry. Pull over."

JESS WAITED BY THE phone for word of her mother. The police had told her the best thing she could do was to stay put. But, with the furious storm outside, it was hard to keep from running into the gale and dashing wildly along the street in a mad search for her confused and stubborn parent, who at this very moment could be freezing to death in some alley.

Since the retreat, Mamie had become more and more bewildered and contrary. Jess had tried to interest her in some hobby or other, even a gourmet cooking class. *Anything.* Nothing seemed to hold her interest. And yesterday Jess had awakened to find Mamie had disappeared.

Jess hadn't slept all night. If she were to be honest, she hadn't had much rest ever since Lucas had walked into—then out of—her life. She was exhausted, terrified and at her wit's end.

Hearing a sound outside, she started. Was it a car engine? Maybe the police had found her mother and were bringing her back. Hope surging through her, she rushed to the front door and flung it wide. Snow stung her eyes and she blinked and squinted, trying to see through the howling wall of white. It wasn't a police car, but a long black limousine. Unfolding himself from the back, was a handsome figure dressed in a charcoal gray suit. As he strode toward her front porch, his hawklike features came into view, as classic and riveting as she remembered. Lucas!

What was he doing here? Jess felt her heart lurch with foolish longing. She was so alone, so frightened. If only he were there to enfold her in his arms, tell her everything was all right. "Lucas?" she whispered in disbelief, he took the porch steps two at a time.

Grabbing her by the hand, he said, "Come with me," and all but dragged her away.

Fifteen minutes later in growing dusk, they were creeping down a narrow section road in a deep wood. Because of the tree cover, there was only a light powdering of snow on the dirt lane.

"Do you really think she might be there? Mother only saw it that once, on the hayride," Jess ventured. The trip had been awkwardly quiet. Lucas's stern expression discouraged idle chatter. He'd sat in brooding silence, as though he were fighting some internal battle. Now she watched his stark profile, fearful, waiting for him to respond.

Lucas had told her that just as they'd driven up to her house to offer to help, the car phone had rung. It had been Maxim, relaying a message from Jack, that when he'd gone in search of Moron, he'd seen smoke coming from the cottage chimney. Lucas had thought it might be Mamie.

"We'll know soon enough," he answered finally, startling Jess from her thoughts. Jerry pulled to a halt. "Through those trees. Here." He lifted his cashmere overcoat and indicated that she put it on. "The cottage is about a hundred yards up that path."

She slid her arms into the huge, soft coat as Jerry opened her door. She and Lucas hurried up the barely discernible trail. Luckily, she was wearing jeans and tennis shoes, so the going was easy, even over the uneven terrain.

Hoping against hope, Jess ran on ahead and burst open the door. Inside she was met by an outlandish sight. Mamie sat on the horse-blanketed couch, a china tea service before her on the small table. Jack was beside her, holding a mug. A wet dog sprawled contentedly before a blazing fire. Nearby sat a washtub filled with a murky red substance.

Mamie peered at them, startled by the intrusion. "Well," she admonished, "You two are late. We've gone ahead without you."

Jess sagged against the wall in relief as Lucas closed the door. "Mother," she managed, through a sigh. "I've been worried sick."

Mamie poured from the pot into Jack's mug. "There you are, dear. Would you care for milk and lemon?"

Jack sipped. "Mrs. Ritter," he replied with a lopsided grin, "it's cocoa."

She tittered. "Oh, my, yes. Silly me." Glowering at Jess, she scolded, "You befuddled me, Jessica. And just what sort of outfit is that? You look like a Secret Service agent with bad dandruff."

Moron sat up and barked, wagging his tail.

"Mother, what are you doing here?" Jess asked, too relieved to be angry.

"Why, I'm having a Summit meeting. This is Boris What's-It and this—" she indicated the dog "—is . . ." She screwed up her face. "Who is this, Boris?" she asked Jack. "My mind's a blank."

"That's a stupid dog," Jack said, looking fondly at the mutt.

"Now, now, Boris," she reproved, taking a sip of her cocoa. "We shall get nowhere *near* world peace with that cheeky attitude. I'll have no name-calling at my Summit."

Jess felt a tug on her arm, and turned to see Lucas looking down at her, doing his best not to smile. "I don't think we have the security clearance for this," he said. "Why don't we go let the police know she's safe?"

Jess nodded, feeling oddly breathless. It was the first time he had smiled at her in so very long. Reluctantly turning away, she called, "Mother, we'll be back later. Okay?"

Mamie waved them off with grandiose impatience. "Go. *Go.* My press secretary will have a statement for you this evening."

"Yeah," Jack added. "He'll bark." With a look that plainly said he thought Mamie was weird, but likable, he took a gulp of his cocoa.

As Jess and Lucas went down the steps, he shouted over the wind, "Looks like she finally got her white house."

Jess shook her head helplessly. "I don't know what I'm going to do with her." Then, facing him, she asked the question that had been plaguing her mind ever since he grabbed her hand on her front porch. "What are you doing here?" Her voice sounded fairly steady, considering her anguished state of mind. "I thought you had a meeting in Tokyo—according to Annie." She lifted her hands to shelter her eyes from the biting snow. "She seems to chat with you on a regular basis, these days."

He took her arm, urging her to the cover of the trees where there was some protection from the storm. "Just twice," he amended. "She talked. I listened." He glanced away, his expression again agitated. It was plain he was at war with himself about his feelings for the kids—his natural sensitivity versus his conscious desire to be thoroughly in command of his heart and his career.

"What happened with Tokyo? Was the trip delayed?" she asked, knowing she shouldn't care, shouldn't involve herself in his life anymore. But she couldn't help it. Lord save her, she *loved* the man.

"No, it wasn't delayed," he said simply. He turned back to face her, and stood, towering over her silently, his arresting eyes filled with unbelievable warmth. The storm seemed to recede into a hushed stillness as they stared at each other. There was no world, no reality beyond the two of them, sheltered beneath a canopy of winter branches in the dwindling twilight.

Finally Lucas took her hands in his and began quietly, "I didn't go to Tokyo today. And I may not have a job tomorrow."

Jess regarded him gravely and prayed that his next words would not extinguish the crazy flicker of hope that had been kindled in her heart by his tender look and the touch of his hands. "I don't understand," she said, but her voice was so weak, she wasn't sure he heard.

With a sudden move, he hauled her into the heat of his arms, and muttered against her cool cheek, "I'm saying, I couldn't go to Tokyo thinking your mother might die, and you'd have to grieve alone. The last year of my grandmother's life, she got confused, wandered off. The day she died— Well, let's say I've been there, and—" He stopped, cleared a thickness from his voice. "I wanted to be with you."

"But—but we found her," she reminded. "You can still go."

He shook his head. "We couldn't take off in this storm," he said. "The important thing is, Mamie's all right." He hugged her more tightly to him, gently rocking her back and forth, comforting her. "Thank God for that."

Relishing this unexpected intimacy they might never share again, Jess clung to him and buried her face against his throat. "Oh, Lucas," she cried. "I'm so sorry about your—"

"Dammit," he growled, cutting her off. "I told you never to apologize to me. *I* made the choice to stay." He stopped abruptly, as though fighting for control, and simply held her nestled against his supple strength. He freed a stray lock of her hair that had become trapped inside his coat, and smoothed it across the gray cashmere collar. When he spoke again, his voice was gentle, but rough with emotion. "Jess, this is hard. But what I'm trying to say is—I love you."

Her heart stumbled perilously. "You—you love me?" she asked, staggered to hear him voice it.

He pressed her away, appraising her with a look that was nearly unbearable in its tenderness. "I do. And I want you to marry me," he added soberly. "I've fought my feelings for you with all my strength, but today, when I heard your mother was missing, I knew I couldn't leave you." A large, gentle hand came up to brush a tear from her cheek. "Of course, if I'm out of your system, I won't embarrass you by mentioning it again."

Their gazes held, and for Jess, there would never be need for another verbal pledge between them. The staggering honesty in his dark eyes conveyed far more commitment than words could ever do. "Oh, Lucas. You'll never be out of my system," she assured him through a trembly sigh. "So, mention it, darling. Mention it over and over...."

He lifted her in his arms and struck off toward the limo. "Sweetheart," he murmured huskily, grazing her cheek with his lips, "as soon as I get you alone, I plan to do a lot more than just mention it."

She grinned at him, deliriously happy. He was smiling at her—really smiling—all lurking doubt and sadness gone from his expression. She stretched up and covered his mouth with hers.

He returned the kiss with all the passion he had so recently held in check, and the depth of emotion left her weak and dizzy. She settled back in his arms, her eyes closed, and reveled in the glory of it. How was this possible? Her prayers had been answered—suddenly and perfectly. This powerful, guarded, unemotional man had risked his career to stay and help her search for her mother! The same unpredictable, sometimes-irrational woman her ex-husband had called loony tunes! How could she ever have thought of Lucas as anything but the most sensitive, caring—*nicest guy*—in the world?

Snuggling within his embrace, she kissed his throat, and teased, "Could you enjoy making love to me as much as working in your Virtual Reality world?"

He flashed a mischievous grin. "Bottom line?"

She nodded, her lips still throbbing from his sizzling kiss.

With a sexy chuckle, he nuzzled her cheek, crooning near her ear, "Stick with me, baby, and one day we'll make love on the rings of Saturn."

Jess felt the joy of utter completeness, absolutely sure that they would.

Epilogue

As Jess and Lucas entered his hospital room, Norman Roxbury glanced up from his book and beamed in surprise. She thought he looked much better today. There was new color in the elderly man's cheeks, and he'd gained some needed weight. "I can see you're feeling better, Norman," she said, as she and Lucas came over to stand beside his bed. Leaning down, she gave him a kiss on the cheek.

He grinned that elfish grin. "Finally taught the chef to make a proper blueberry flapjack."

Lucas chuckled, dropped an arm about Jess's shoulder and drew her close. Jess still could not quite believe her good fortune. Had it only been two days ago that Lucas had proposed? So much had happened since then.

Lucas had insisted on taking a six-month leave of absence for an extended honeymoon. Then, to Jess's amazement, he'd installed a glowing Mamie in his home as his "executive assistant." It meant she had a phone, an office, and accounts at local florist, stationery and gourmet-food shops. Her duties were minimal. She was to keep their social schedule straight and play hostess when business meetings were held at the house. If Jess hadn't already loved Lucas with all her heart, she would have loved him solely for what he'd done for her mother.

Not only that. When Takahashi had learned the reason Lucas had missed the Tokyo meeting, he'd rescheduled. It seemed the Japanese drug tycoon had a particular soft spot for his own aging mother, and thought Lucas's reason for dropping out was highly noble. Sol would attend the meeting in Lucas's place, however. In a week, he'd be fine.

"Well, my boy," Norman was saying, "you look pretty fit. A little tired, perhaps. And I don't believe I've seen you in jeans since you were a boy." He laced his fingers behind his head, and added, "I understand the Thanksgiving Retreat went off nicely. I want to thank you for your help." Jess noticed he was taking careful note of the possessive arm about her shoulders, and his eyes began to glisten. "Did anything happen I should know about?"

"Nothing you didn't plan, you old devil," Lucas admonished with a chuckle. "But I want to thank you for your meddling."

Norman laughed, and the sound of it was heartier than it had been in a long time. "My boy," he offered sheepishly, "forgive an old man his wiliness. But I've always loved you as a son, and I've grown to love Jess like a daughter." He shrugged thin shoulders. "Seemed only natural to get you two together."

Jess bent down and kissed him again. "We're grateful, Norman. More than we could ever repay." She straightened and smiled lovingly at the wonderful man she'd met right here in this room. "Lucas and I have something for you, Norman."

The old man's bushy eyebrows rose in question. "Oh? What is it?"

"Your doctor tells us you'll be well enough to travel by New Year's." Lucas pulled an airline ticket from his breast pocket. "So, we want to thank you for pushing us together by sending you to visit your niece and her twins, in Hawaii."

Norman's surprise was evident. "Why, I— That's fine of you both," he said. "I'd love to see Lucia and the children, but don't forget I have the Senior Citizens' New Year's Eve Party to plan."

Jess grinned down at him. "Lucas and I will handle it." She reached up to squeeze the large hand that rested on her arm. "We thought we'd help you out with that, and the Teenage Mothers' Camp every summer. Along with the Mr. Niceguy program, of course."

Jess was touched to see tears form in the old man's eyes. He settled back against his pillow, looking happy and at peace. "I'll accept that, gladly. I've been thinking of semiretiring. Your offer is a great weight off my mind." He looked at Lucas, his gaze shining with affection. "But I have to say, my boy, the best gift you've given me is seeing you regain that wonderful compassion of your youth. That was my true hope." He indicated the sparkling diamond engagement ring on Jess's left hand. "And I'd be lying if I didn't admit I was rooting for this, too. When's the wedding?"

Jess smiled, feeling suddenly shy and terribly blessed. "Christmas Day. And it wouldn't be complete if you didn't give me away."

"My dear child," Norman said, with a mischievous wink, "I did *that* the day Lucas walked into this room and met you." He chuckled. "But, of course, I will be happy to oblige. Couldn't ask for better incentive to get back on these old legs."

ON THE WAY HOME in the limo, Jess snuggled into the sheltering warmth of her fiancé's arms. She sighed contentedly. "It seems you're the official Mr. Niceguy from now on. Happy?"

"Very. But, I'd think being married to Mr. Niceguy would bother you," he murmured, rubbing a finger seductively along her jaw. "After all, as the saying goes, Nice Guys Finish Last."

She shifted in his arms, and her tongue teased his earlobe, as she said softly, "Ah, but I've found that to be a 'stroke' of luck if you happen to be making love."

He flashed an all-too-sexy grin that sent her world careening crazily around her. Her only reality became his heady scent and the exquisite passion in his dark eyes. "Unfortunately," he reminded in a low, husky tone, "we don't happen to be making love."

With lighthearted abandon, Jess closed the shade between the driver and the passenger area. She slid her arms about his neck and drew his lips down to graze hers, coaxing, "Want to make a bet—Mr. Niceguy?"

SUMMER SPECIAL!

Four exciting new Romances for the price of three

Each Romance features British heroines and their encounters with dark and desirable Mediterranean men. *Plus, a free Elmlea recipe booklet inside every pack.*

So sit back and enjoy your sumptuous summer reading pack and indulge yourself with the free Elmlea recipe ideas.

Available July 1994   Price £5.70

MILLS & BOON

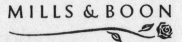

Available from WH Smith, John Menzies, Volume One, Forbuoys, Martins, Woolworths, Tesco, Asda, Safeway and other paperback stockists. Also available from Mills & Boon Reader Service, FREEPOST, PO Box 236, Croydon, Surrey CR9 9EL. (UK Postage & Packing free)

THREE TIMES A LOVE STORY

A special collection of three individual love stories from one of the world's best-loved romance authors. This beautiful volume offers a unique chance for new fans to sample some of Janet Dailey's earlier works and for long-time fans to collect an edition to treasure.

W⊙RLDWIDE

AVAILABLE NOW   PRICED £4.99

Available from WH Smith, John Menzies, Volume One, Forbuoys, Martins, Woolworths, Tesco, Asda, Safeway and other paperback stockists. Also available from Worldwide Reader Service, FREEPOST, PO Box 236, Croydon, Surrey CR9 9EL. (UK Postage & Packing free)

This month's
irresistible novels from

Temptation

NIGHT WATCH by Carla Neggers
Live the fantasy...in Lovers and Legends

Once upon a time there was a beautiful, reclusive woman who needed to let down her hair—or so the story goes. Burned-out cop Joe Scarlatti had a gut feeling that Rowena Willow was in grave danger. She had testified against a slick con artist and now he was out of jail...and out to get her!

NO MORE MR. NICE by Renee Roszel
Forced to play Mr. Nice-Guy was not Lucas Brand's idea of fun. Determined to resent every single second of helping Jess Glen, Lucas surprised himself when it turned out that he did have a way with kids...

MANHUNTING by Jennifer Crusie
Kate Svenson knew *exactly* what she wanted in a man—he had to be tall, handsome, distinguished and, most of all, successful. So she went on a serious manhunting excursion determined to hunt down Mr. Right—or die in the attempt!

THE SHERIFF OF DEVIL'S FORK by Regan Forest
Jake MacGuire was determined, tormented...lonely. Law and order was his creed—not romance. Dana French had no idea what she was letting herself in for when she inherited her great-aunt's house in Devil's Fork. Her legacy held an incredible secret. Would she ever be able to reveal the truth to Jake...and how she had learned it?

Available from W H Smith, John Menzies, Volume One, Forbuoys, Martins, Woolworths, Tesco, Asda, Safeway and other paperback stockists. Also available from Mills & Boon Reader Service, FREEPOST, P.O. Box 236, Croydon, Surrey CR9 9EL. (UK Postage & Packing free).

Spoil yourself next month
with these four novels from

Temptation

NAUGHTY TALK by Tiffany White
Live the fantasy...in Lovers and Legends

*Once upon a time a handsome knight errant went searching for
the secrets of women's deepest desires*—or so the story goes.
Nicole Hart wanted revenge on Anthony Gawain.
Masquerading as a provocative sex therapist on his TV show
presented just the opportunity Nicole needed to teach him a
thing or two...

JUST THE WAY YOU ARE by Elise Title

Why had she married uptight Mike Powell? But the minute
Lucy had signed the divorce decree she was sorry. Mike had
had it with his wife's fiery temper. But now they were parting
he remembered just how vivacious and sultry she could be.
What lengths would they go to to get back together again?

DECEPTIONS by Janice Kaiser

As a teenager, Darcy Hunter was guiltily infatuated with her
older sister's fiancé, Kyle Weston. Following her sister's tragic
death, Kyle dropped out of Darcy's life—but not fully out of
her heart and fantasies. What would she do now that she was
being drawn back into his dangerous circuit?

SEEING RED by Roseanne Williams

When Larinda Outlaw inherited a run-down business, she
thought her dreams had come true. Now she could get hold of
some cold, hard cash. Instead she got hot, sexy Cash Bowman
who stood in the way of her plans to sell.

Proudly present...

CHARLOTTE LAMB'S
♥ *100th* ♥
ROMANCE

This is a remarkable achievement for a writer who had her first Mills & Boon novel published in 1973. Some six million words later and with sales around the world, her novels continue to be popular with romance fans everywhere.

Her centenary romance '*VAMPIRE LOVER*' is a suspense-filled story of dark desires and tangled emotions—Charlotte Lamb at her very best.

Published: June 1994   Price: £1.90

Available from WH Smith, John Menzies, Volume One, Forbuoys, Martins, Woolworths, Tesco, Asda, Safeway and other paperback stockists. Also available from Mills & Boon Reader Service, FREEPOST, PO Box 236, Croydon, Surrey CR9 9EL (UK Postage & Packing free).